JOY, JOY, WHY DO I SING?

JOY, JOY, WHY DO I SING?

DARLENE MADOTT

WOMEN'S PRESS
TORONTO

Joy, Joy, Why Do I Sing?
Darlene Madott

First published in 2004 by
Women's Press, an imprint of Canadian Scholars' Press Inc.
180 Bloor Street West, Suite 801
Toronto, Ontario
M5S 2V6

www.womenspress.ca

Canadian Scholars' Press/Women's Press gratefully acknowledges financial support for our publishing activities from the Ontario Arts Council, the Canada Council for the Arts, and the Government of Canada through the Book Publishing Industry Development Program (BPIDP).

National Library of Canada Cataloguing in Publication

Madott, Darlene
Joy, joy, why do I sing? / Darlene Madott.
ISBN 0-88961-440-7
I. Title.
PS8576.A335J68 2004   C813'.54   C2003-905892-1

Cover and text design by George Kirkpatrick
Cover photo by Jim Avery
Author photo by Jason Schwartz

04   05   06   07   08   6   5   4   3   2   1

Printed and bound in Canada by AGMV Marquis Imprimeur, Inc.

This book is for Marcus. On your third day of life, I looked down at you through worried tears as to whether I would be able to feed you, when you, looking up into your mother's face with blind eyes, gave me your first smile. That smile absolved me. For it and you, I am eternally grateful.

table of contents

acknowledgements

"Extract of the Piano Lesson Concerning Chopin's C Sharp Minor Étude" and "Epilogue" are extracts from *Song and Silence*, by Darlene Madott, Borealis Press, 1977. Reprinted by permission of Borealis Press Ltd.

"Waiting" originally appeared in *Bottled Roses*, by Darlene Madott, Oberon Press, 1985. Reprinted by permission of the author.

"The Question" originally appeared in *The Capilano Review*: The Capilano Press Society, Fall 1994. © Darlene Madott.

"The Superintendent" originally appeared in *The Toronto Star*, July 12, 1988. © Darlene Madott.

"Unwanted Gifts" originally appeared in the *Wascana Review of Contemporary Poetry*. © Darlene Madott.

"The Caller" originally appeared in *The Toronto Star*, July 11, 1988. © Darlene Madott.

"A Promise to Noma Miller" originally appeared in *Grain Magazine*: Saskatchewan Writers' Guild, 1976. © Darlene Madott.

Lyric excerpts in "Joy, Joy, Why Do I Sing" are from Leon Dubinsky, *We Rise Again* (VA-2005): Shagrock Music, 1985. Reprinted by permission of Leon Dubinsky.

ode to a single child

I watch from the kitchen window
as he serves to himself,
then pivots wildly, running backward, and swings,
returning the birdie…

How long can this last?

My heart, washing dishes,
cries with the question he will only
ask years later,
borne of the same desperate loneliness
with which I had him:

"Why did you have me?
Why did you have only me?"

"You were so special, I could not
imagine doing any better…
A second time;
I loved you so much, I could
Not conceive of sharing what I felt for you,
With any other…."

And then the words I cannot say:

When I was forty, when it would have been
time,
when I should have—
your father and I…
I could not do that to another child…
bring him into a world knowing his parents were
separating.

Maybe it would have been better for you.
At least you would not have had to
go through this alone, but
I did not see it that way, at the time…

"You had me too late;
You should not have done that,
At thirty-seven…"

How do I tell him?

Gifts can never be
too late?

My courageous, single child—

You were just in time.

extract of the piano lesson concerning Chopin's C sharp minor étude:

"I don't like the way you played the first phrase...you seem to sit on that first note. I know Chopin marked it a quarter and the tempo is *lento*, but you have got to make it to the second note, cheat the note values a little, anticipate the second note, and incidentally, a big accent on it when you land. It's a poignant moment. One note in isolation means nothing. It communicates nothing. It's the interval, the relationship between two notes and how you move from one to the other that creates an emotion. In this case it's the interval of a fifth. Well, make it leap. One note vibrating alone has no power to move you or me unless it is joined to another note to establish some kind of relationship between them. Make them sing together."

Effortlessly, he played the first phrase. The music lifted out from under the touch of his fingers and filled the room. He played it very slowly, with great sadness and great simplicity. Only his hand and wrist moved. His body remained motionless, the shoulders sagged over his sunken chest. His head was bowed, his eyes closed, and his chin almost touched his chest. His free right hand rested limply on his knee. As he played he made a rough sound inside his throat, almost a moan, which seemed to force its way out of him as he felt the music rise inside.

When he played the phrase a second time, on sounding the second note, he lifted the palm of his right hand in the air and the upturned fingers shook in emphasis. He turned his head on its side and strained his ear toward the keys. Then he repeated just those two notes again, this time looking at Danielle as if to graft the sounds onto her mind, raising his eyebrows as the music lifted again toward the second note, his body articulating his thoughts....

"Do you hear it?"

Now, with seasons of time between herself and that moment, Danielle *heard*.

One note in isolation has no meaning. It communicates nothing. One note vibrating alone means nothing.

waiting

FRANNY HAD TO find out what it would be like, if her body could respond. Without her. With a stranger. A way of expiating another. She was out of breath when he kissed her, as if she had been running. She told him she was afraid, was on the point of turning back. He said she had nothing to fear: he would not hurt her. Franny told herself: you can't judge the world by one man, by the hand over your mouth the very first time ever.

He never turned on the light in his apartment. They undressed in the dark, so he did not see her hands trembling. She said she had never made love to a man she didn't know. He said, "Probably not to one you knew, either." She heard him chuckle to himself, imagined he laughed with his chin tucked into his chest—either a shy laugh, or very guarded. At least he is intelligent, she thought. That made her feel less ashamed. She tried talking to herself. It was either now or never. But the feeling in her stomach was a kind of drowning. She was fighting for air.

"I don't want to get pregnant," she told him. He said he would take care of that: "Do you think I *want* to make you pregnant?" He said it so forcefully, Franny wondered what he meant, assumed he must be alluding to something in his past. It was one of those intimations of a person that never make sense until later, often not until it is too late.

She tried very hard. Then she gave up and lay under him in a kind of panic, waiting for it to end. She tried to deaden all feeling, to concentrate on something else, but the panic caught up with her. He withdrew that time without ever coming. She was almost grateful to him. Was he a kind man? Maybe. Maybe not. She asked if he was angry. He drew his hand down across his eyes and lower face, like a man after he shaves, or a man when he is very tired. "It never is good the first time," he said. "Our bodies need more time to get acquainted. We must give them more time."

Franny thought, I will not give you time. I will not let you touch me.

She fully intended never to see him again.

When he called the next morning, there was a new smell blowing through the open window, the fresh smell of cut sweet grass. She was all invention that morning. She told him she thought she was pregnant; she had seen her husband just the once before she left, and they had made love. She actually said this to frighten him off, so that he would not trouble her again. Unexpectedly, her lie drew him closer. He offered to help. It was not his problem, she said. He asked if she still loved her husband, if it would force her back to him if her fears turned out to be real. It seems so unbelievable now that she should have considered the question seriously all summer, as if it were a real possibility.

Was any of it real? She remembered waking somewhere in the night to the panic of railcars being severed and attached. She had turned on her side to watch the dark line of sleep spread through the mountains like the breasts of a reclining woman. Running away can be exhilarating at first, but then endless as certain dreams, and just as unreal. That whole summer turned into a kind of waiting. A waiting to return. A waiting to bleed. For she really did not get her period. Something had dried up in her.

When Franny did return that August, her sister would say she looked haunted. She was thin as a rake. She would say that when she hugged Franny at the train station, her whole body had stiffened; she had not wanted to be touched.

Franny did not let him touch her. She carried another inside her the whole length of the route. Was it any wonder she came to believe in the little child she felt certain was in her, the child that—had love lasted—she would most certainly have had?

He set the whole day aside for her. They started off in the morning with breakfast at a restaurant overlooking the sea. Then he took her to the Aquarium, where she saw for the first time these beautiful coloured creatures that blossomed before her eyes like underwater fireworks. He told her their name—anemones—his eyes watching her lips as she repeated it. He never looked into her eyes.

Then he took her for a drive along the North Shore. He did not speak, and Franny lay back in the seat and let her eyes close.

She had never known a more silent man. In the car that day his silence had angered her. She thought it wilful, like the silence with which her husband used to punish her. She resolved not to care. But she felt hostile nonetheless. So she interrogated him. What did he want from life? Who was he? What did he do for a living? What did he have to say for himself?

He said nothing. And then nothing. He was resolute about this silence of his. She felt her face flush with anger. She told him that his silence was like that of a peasant — without expectation. He looked at her with surprise. He looked about to say something, but she saw him change his mind. So she lay back in the seat and resolved to forget about him. With the windows fully open and the air so warm, she must have dozed. They stopped only twice, once to take a path through the rainforest, and then to explore a small fishing village where he bought her ice cream. By the time they arrived back that evening, her face was burnt from the sun and sea air, and she was starving.

Hours after she had asked the question and forgotten it, he attempted an answer. He said his one ambition in life, before he knew better, had been to own one of those homes they had seen along the North Shore, to be a millionaire by thirty. He hadn't a doubt he could have done it. He told her that when he was a teenager, he had bought a rowboat with a small motor and used to spend his Sundays gazing up at the cliffs, at the homes that looked, not down at him bobbing in the sea, but out at nothing, their windows as if blinded. A false dream. Like most desire, he said. He knew better at thirty. She wondered what had happened in his life to make him so unexpectant?

He ordered something not on the menu, something she had never tasted before—white bean cakes in a delicate sauce, with flakes of green ginger. As each dish came to their table, he served the food onto her plate, as if to make sure that she was eating enough. It seemed such a caring gesture. But he did it without thinking, as if this were a long habit of his, to fill the plates of the people with whom he ate. It was such an odd thing, the way he'd remark about this or that, and spoon food onto her plate—she was thoroughly charmed. The bean cakes tasted like air, like she was feeding on air. She touched his ankle with her sandaled foot. She told him she had not felt any hunger in weeks. He had given her back her appetite. That seemed to please him. He grasped her foot between his two and held it there. Every now and then she would try to pull it back, but he would anticipate the tug, like a fish on a hook, and not let her go.

Above the table, they were utter strangers. He never took her hand, hardly spoke. His pale eyes looked always down, always away from her. She thought, he is not an easy man. He does not seem to need anything.

"Look at me," she said.

He would not look at her. His eyes were a pale blue, almost white. They looked at some distant point over her shoulder. He reached down and put his warm hand around her foot, between the instep and the sandal. Then he gave the foot a tug, so that, like a bobbin on water, her body dipped down at the tug. She clutched the table for support and laughed like a schoolgirl at how silly that must have looked. His strange affection pleased her. But she would not be deterred.

"I know nothing about you."

"What do you need to know?"

"Who you are, what you do."

He said, "You can't judge a man by what he does for a living."

She thought, then: it must be something that embarrasses him.

"You've told me nothing about your past."

There was a pause. He said he wanted to stop at a bakery before taking her home. He was going to buy her cakes for her breakfast the next morning. He had noticed she was too thin. He risked a glance in her direction and chuckled. She saw that she was right about his laugh—that he laughed inward, with his chin tucked into his chest. She saw the pain she could cause with her questions.

"Why aren't you married?"

"I don't need a wife," he said. "I can do everything for myself." The directness of his answer made her laugh.

Was that all a wife meant?

He was just giving her fair warning. They might be lovers, but he was not going to marry her.

At that she really laughed. Not to worry, she said. She had no *designs* upon him. She would not marry him if he begged her. In any case, she would be gone in a few months.

Franny let herself out of the car and slammed the door. His startled face, hand holding out the box of pastries. She did not take his box of pastries.

They existed together like that in a kind of flat present tense. She understood that what he needed was someone for whom he did not have any past. Perhaps she needed that too. For she consented to be with him, a passenger in his present, in his silence.

One day they met where the trolleys loop in Stanley Park, and made the seven-mile walk around the seawall together. They had not brought their bathing suits or towels. At Second Beach, she lay back in the sand, overcome by the heat, and he half-sat, half-lay beside her, his hand under her head so that her long hair would not fill with sand.

He said she was not pregnant. She did not have the look of a pregnant woman. Her body was just upset. It could be anything, he said—the journey out. He touched her stomach through her sundress and told her to stop worrying, there was nothing *in* there.

The dress she was wearing was a pale blue cotton with thin shoulder straps. It had a full skirt, and she loved the freedom of walking in it. She had loved that dress, the way the wind would catch it and wrap it around her legs. She had bought it for her honeymoon. It was one of those dresses she could never bring herself to throw out. As she lay there on the sand, she was trying to remember why her husband had hated it.

Through the cotton, the hand felt warm and comforting, like the touch of a father. She put her hand over his hand to keep him there.

"What does a pregnant woman look like?" she asked. It sounded like a riddle, or the beginning of a joke.

"Half asleep," he said. "She has a stillness you do not possess, a cloud over the eyes, like a fish sleeping."

"How do you know what a pregnant woman looks like?"

"I know," he said simply.

Franny showered off the sand and dressed in one of his shirts, and took the glass of wine he gave her. He kept white wine in his fridge, even though he himself didn't drink. He had made a resolution about drinking. It was one of those conclusions about his life for which there was never any explanation. The blinds were drawn, and the sun had turned the room brown through the slats. It was very hot in his room, the glass so cold; Franny drank from it thirstily.

They made love easily that time. She cried out when she came, and her cry must have startled him, for he stopped suddenly and asked if he was hurting her.

No, she managed, using the broken language of lovers.

Afterward, he lay on his back in a softened mood, his guard down. She saw the bruise-like marks on his body. He told her he had once been a welder. He described the pain in his eyes whenever he had accidentally stared at the flame too long. It was a pain that came to life only hours later, would begin toward evening and increase steadily into the night. There was nothing he could do for it, he said, except cold teabags. He had always kept wet teabags in his fridge.

Franny started to cry. Not for the pain, for his description of the pain—an insidious pain that announced itself only after the damage was done. He picked her up and carried her to a chair and sat with her on his knee.

"What will I do? What am I going to do?"

"With your life, you mean, or the next minute?"

"What will I do?"

He kissed her thoughtfully.

"Have you ever considered keeping your baby, if it turns out to be real?"

"Why do you want to be with me? I'm no fun to be with."

"I want to be with you," he said simply.

"Tell me what you most don't like about me."

"I like everything about you," he said.

"There must be something," Franny suggested. "My eyebrows? My voice?"

"I love your voice."

"My husband hated my voice," she said quietly.

There was a silence. It settled between them, making the afternoon almost fibrous.

"Has it ever occurred to you that maybe you were never the woman he thought he wanted, that maybe he didn't know what he wanted?"

"It didn't have to turn out the way it did. I loved him, you know." She felt foolish, telling that to a lover.

"You know what you have to do with thoughts like that? You put them in this no-way-of-ever-knowing box for when you've got nothing better to do. Right now, you've got something better."

He gave her a hug and patted her back.

"What will I do? What am I going to do?"

"Stay," he said, "and figure it out." He made her smile, then: "You want teabags for those eyes?"

Gradually, imperceptibly, he became necessary. He was always there, someone else, someone with his own separate and impenetrable world. He asked nothing of her. There were the days she did not see him, and then the days she did. The days he said he could not see her, she imagined all sorts of things. She imagined he was a prisoner out on parole. The thought that he might once have done something violent frightened her, though she felt certain he would never hurt her.

"I didn't know until yesterday that I would miss you," she said to him one day.

They had rolled up their jeans and waded out to a rock off Second Beach to watch the setting sun. The incoming tide drew an ever closer ring around them on the rock. For once their faces were in harmony, painted the same Indian red. Across from them in the harbour, strings of coloured lights suddenly lit the masts of the tall ships moored there.

"Will you miss me when I'm gone?"

"I can take care of myself," he said.

"Can you?"

"Can *you*?" he answered, and she was startled by the edge in his voice.

Yesterday had been one of the days he could not see her. Franny had spent it wandering around Chinatown, buying gifts for her family against her return. Sooner or later, she would have to return. It was the only thing that summer of which she was certain. She had just left a bakery, carrying a box of assorted pastries, when across the street she thought she saw him waiting for the light to change. He was with a woman. She started to run. She crushed the box of pastries against the old lady blocking her path. A horn screamed at the intersection. She grabbed his forearm and spun him around. There wasn't even a resemblance. Afterward, she had to lean against a building to catch her breath, tears filling up the whole moon of her eyes. She felt suddenly sickened. It had not even occurred to her that he might betray her in that way.

"I wasn't in Chinatown yesterday."

"I'm glad," she said. "You were with a woman."

"It isn't anything like that."

From across the water, they heard the low mournful whistle of a train. It was strangely beckoning. The tide was forcing them from their rock, which, anyway, had begun to grow cold.

"Is *he* what is forcing you back?" he asked, finally.

Franny picked a direction. Their evening walks always began in this way. Off they would go, wandering through districts that reminded her of her childhood, around corner stores and down laneways where as a kid she might have hunted Popsicle sticks and pop bottles. They would always end up in some restaurant, for he always insisted on feeding her. This one had plastic grapes hanging from the ceiling along with last year's Christmas decorations. They decided on a pizza, while the owner went next door to buy the soft drinks they had ordered. They pumped the jukebox full of quarters and pressed buttons at random, laughing at the unlikely juxtapositions — the Neapolitan lovesongs, followed by Elvis Presley. Franny wanted to dance. There was no one else in the restaurant. But in this he would not oblige her. "Please," he said, looking alarmed, as she tried to pull him to his feet.

Midsummer night, they went swimming.

"You'll leave me suddenly," he said. "You'll leave me with-out warning. You won't leave me enough memories."

They had taken a shortcut through a summer schoolyard, their wet bathing suits rolled in the same towel. Lovers for three weeks, they were both three weeks behind on their laundry. When she told him, "I can't see you tonight, I have to do my laundry," he had wanted to do it together. "Bring it over here, and we'll do it together." "Are you serious?" she said. "My dirty underwear spinning around in there with yours?"

Their bathing suits would leave a humid little patch on the wood bleacher when they were gone. They sat together and gazed at the moon. She said, let's plan to meet someday in Barcelona.

"We will never meet in Barcelona. The timing will always be off. One of us would either arrive too soon or too late, at the wrong corner, the wrong night…."

He wanted to take her to the market. They would buy a whole salmon and he would show her how to salt it. If she could wait until late August, they might take a holiday together. They could hike into the mountains and pitch a tent beside a lake, or he would rent a cabin if she preferred. There were so many things still to do yet.

"You're not leaving me with enough memories. We haven't made enough memories."

A memory: the night of fireworks at English Bay. He said they would be able to watch from his balcony. Franny had a fever. There were white spots lining her throat. For weeks now she had been waking with a weight on her chest, her throat constricted and flaming. He listened to the symptoms, and then he said, "You have homesickness. In your mind, you are already leaving me." He wrapped her in a sweater, even though it was July. He made a cup of tea and brought it out to her on the balcony, with two aspirins. She took the aspirins in her palm. They were very small and pink. She sat on the chair next to him, with her legs over his, watching the crowds converge toward the bay. He bent over and kissed her knees. He said he loved the smell of her knees, like two sweet flowers. Then he reached over and folded her in. He kissed her deeply. She did not want him to kiss her that way because of the white sores on her throat. She turned her mouth away. He crushed an aspirin and placed its powder on the tip of his little finger, and touched the spots inside her throat. He kissed her again.

They made love quickly, both coming at the same instant. He looked down to where she curled under him like a small burning animal. He just looked at her. "What?" she asked. He just looked at her, as if memorizing her face.

Afterwards, they went swimming under the humid sky. With the city's populace at English Bay for the opening of the Sea Festival, they had the rooftop pool to themselves. Fireworks began exploding, shattering the warm blackness into a thousand stars. Each wave caught a glint of it and dispersed light, a handful of stars, so that they were surrounded by a galaxy. There are moments in life when the pleasure is almost more than one can bear. Franny felt as if two hands had taken hold of something in her chest and were squeezing it, ever so slightly. With each gentle pressure, she lost her breath. He held her. He held *onto* her, as if he were afraid she might slip under and drown; he might lose her in the black space between lights. While she gazed up at the fireworks, he looked down at her face. "Oh, look," she said. "Yes, look at you," he said. But the rest was lost in a wonder of explosions. He found her mouth and kissed her for as long as they lasted.

That night, he broke silence. Like the closed anemone, he suddenly opened, extending himself out. He told her he had a son.

"Why didn't you tell me sooner?"

"I am telling you now."

"Now is too late."

"I'm glad it's too late."

"It's as if you had lied to me. Why didn't you tell me?"

"You were always going," he said. "I always knew you would leave me in the end. There never seemed to be any point."

"Why now, then? What has made the difference?"

He said nothing. He looked away. He looked like a man condemned and waiting for the sentence.

What will you do if it turns out to be real? Have you ever considered keeping your baby?

Suddenly, the meaning of everything became clear—from the days spent away from her, to the children's aspirins he had so recently placed in her hand—what, for a month now, he had kept guarded in silence.

Why did he suddenly mean so much to her, this silent, difficult man, as if not to be able to care now would be a sorrow in itself? She touched his face and he looked up at her.

II

"Hold me," the child demands, whose father has never asked anything of her, who makes no demands.

Franny makes an armchair of her body, and lets her chin come to rest on his wet little shoulder, to see the waves as he sees them, to see if he will let her. What choice does he have? He is just four years old and this is his first time in the ocean, and what little courage he has to face the waves alone, how he paws the air behind him for her with his fierce little hands. Franny puts her arms around his waist and makes a shell of her body. From his height, the waves look so huge and darkening, and for an hour now have been too much. And he wants back to the shore and once there wants the ocean again, and when she gives the ocean back to him, he is sick on his excitement and yearns for the shore, and no sooner there....

Fickle, his father says, like his mother.

You shouldn't say that. He hears, you know. He will never forget.

"Kick," Franny shouts. "Kick hard and ride with it." The boy stiffens and pulls his little chicken's breast out of the water, hanging from her hands. Her back aches with his new weight. He shrieks ecstatically as he bicycles over the next wave, thinking he did it all on his own. Like his father. *Like his father. I can take care of myself.*

Throughout the afternoon, older women have smiled, and Franny smiles back, accepting a guilty maternity. There is a man on the shore—a man who knows, who has been watching her all afternoon.

"Why don't you take off your dark glasses and come in?" The child's questions give everything away. Franny is wearing a green and yellow kerchief wrapped around her hair, to match the green bathing suit. She keeps her head out of the water.

"I am in, sweetheart."

The child still has not looked at her.

For some reason, his father has not brought his bathing suit. Franny sends him back to the apartment to fetch it. His son's first swim in the ocean. This is too important to miss. They promise to wait the twenty minutes out on the sand. She will not let his son swim in the ocean. Together they will sit on this towel. She will teach him how to build sandcastles.

No sooner has the father dropped out of sight than Franny wants to ply the son with questions. What did your daddy make you for breakfast this morning? Where did he take you last week? Do you like being with your daddy? What is it like?

The child kicks sand with his heel. He edges away from the towel. There is no containing him. To that log, Franny tells him, and no farther. He pretends not to hear. At this instant, he is picking a wet string of seaweed from the sand and shaking it out like a tail, and the next he will be indistinguishable from the crowd of colourful sunbathers. She is sick with anxiety. For just a moment she seeks his father on the shore, and the next wave has flattened him. The boy is more shocked than harmed, has only swallowed some water. She sweeps him up in her arms. Upright on the sand, his face has gone alarmingly blank, emptied almost, and then the whole weight of the day crests in a soul-shattering scream. She watches him turn red, little ribs pumping, face pulled into one convulsive knot. Just as suddenly, the sound stops, displaced by that unearthly stillness she finds so disturbing in his father.

"He's had enough," his father says. He stands beside them. The son shoots off across the sand.

And Franny is suddenly so tired, she wants only to lie down, to curl up on the sand, to let the sun bake her.

"Tell me something," she says.

"Stay," he says, "don't go yet."

Franny leaves them shaking sand out of their towels, and walks to the women's change house. The man who has been watching her all afternoon looks up as she passes. He has the eyes and grin of a blackmailer. Franny stares at him murderously and the eyes slide away.

"Down, Daddy, please...please, Daddy."

They have caught up to her, the boy dressed hastily in a T-shirt and white sun hat, bouncing helplessly on his father's shoulders, clutching his dad's hair, while the father, slung with towels and running shoes and cameras and pants, holds him down by the ankles. They look like a ship in full sail, the ropes and canvas not fully battened down yet.

She touches his arm. The ship comes to rest.

"You don't like it up there, do you, sweetheart?"

"No." The voice is almost too quiet.

"So what do we do now? Would you both like some ice cream?"

"Let him down. He's miserable up there."

He lets the boy scramble down from his shoulders. The son stands apart from them, at an unforgiving little distance. Not a twitch. It is as if one move might draw attention to himself and land him right back up on his father's shoulders.

"So what do we do now?" the father asks uncertainly.

Franny stares at the back of the little white sun hat, and presses her forehead with her palm. "I need shade," she says. "Let's find a tree."

They are sitting on a park bench beneath a huge tree. It has great outspreading branches, and Franny is so grateful for its green, for its solidity, she has an impulse to reach out and pat its bark. They sit facing the street, trying to decide what to do. She can hardly think. Bone-weary she is, with an ache in her back that seems pulling her to earth. It suddenly occurs to her that the boy is not moving, not tugging at anything, not running off to be fetched back. He is just sitting there along with them, facing the street.

"You see that bus stop?" His father explains, "He thinks we're waiting for a bus."

Franny bursts out laughing.

"Do you mean that's all you have to do to get him to stay still? Find a bus stop and pretend to be waiting?"

"So what do we do now?"

Now they were waiting. They were, all three of them, waiting. The boy was waiting for the bus. His father was waiting for Franny. And she was waiting for…something. She didn't know what.

"I have to buy my train ticket today."

The train station is like something in a dream. There are so many people, all trying to leave town, and nothing available on any of the days she thought to travel.

"I don't believe I am doing this," he says, as he dials the number for CN, the alternate route. For some reason Franny has not been able to get through; she keeps dialling the wrong number.

"Doesn't it tell you something?" he asks. "Or aren't you listening?"

"So I'll get a ticket for the first available day, or I'll go by coach and not a sleeper. Nothing says I have to leave on a Saturday or Sunday, or any other day of the week. I have nothing to hold me."

He hangs up the phone and catches her. "Am I nothing?" As suddenly as the tears start, they have stopped. She wipes her face on his shirt and looks around for his son. The boy is keeping his usual respectful distance, his back to them both.

"Didn't even notice," she says, and laughs uncomfortably.

"Don't fool yourself," he says, "the little smart ass sees everything."

An hour later, they come back to the spot where Franny has been waiting in line. The boy runs up to her, holding out his new rubber snake.

"Where did you get that, corker?"

"We had hamburgers."

"So is it done?"

"Are you coming to Nanny's with us?" the boy asks, throttling his snake. She pupps down and holds her knees together in a cannonball.

"If it's all the same to you, sweetheart, I think I'll wait outside on the sidewalk."

"Don't be silly," the father says, and grabs one hand from each, one from his son and one from Franny. "How much time do I have?" he asks savagely. "How much time to change your mind?"

"It won't be changed," she tells him. "We have a week."

On the bus to Nanny's Franny teaches the boy how to play "This-little-piggy-went-to-market," only his little piggies prefer spaghetti to roast beef.

"I didn't know you knew those kind of games. I never would have thought it of you." Franny wonders how he perceives her. He is sitting on the aisle seat, legs crossed, arm around them both, making a moon-curve of his body.

"I was a kid once, you know," Franny tells him. "I have a mother."

The boy's little fist bores into her stomach, supporting the whole of his window-gazing weight. She covers the fist with her hand.

To look at them, you might almost think they were a family coming home from the beach, sunburnt and spent.

"Where's his hat?" the father asks suddenly.

The child says nothing. His neck stiffens. Franny sees the blond hairs bristle above his sunburn.

"Your mother bought it?" she asks.

"You know what it looks like—like I haven't been watching, like I don't care...."

When they get off the bus, the child bolts in the direction of a grocery store. His father lets go of Franny's hand.

A woman is pupped down beside a fruit stand, holding out a peeled banana, listening to what the child has to say. Whatever it is, he is telling it wildly. As they approach her, the chatter stops. Her eyes move from the child to his father, and then to Franny.

"I've heard so much about you," she says. Franny is dismayed to think that while she knew nothing of this woman, she has heard all about her.

"You are on holiday?" she asks. "Will you come back, do you think?"

"I don't know," Franny tells her. "I don't know that, at this stage in my life, I want to repeat any experience."

"Even good ones?" the mother asks. She glances at her son, and in her glance Franny sees a mother's worry.

The child tugs at Franny's dress. He is trying to draw her away from the circle of adults to tell her something. His little face is knotted with the effort of communication. He takes her hand, and pulls her out into the yard. It seems his snake is caught up in the tree. As Franny reaches up into the branches, her stomach cramps with the unmistakable pain of her period.

III

It was a masked pregnancy. He had married her too young.

Franny asked him what that meant — "masked pregnancy."

He said it happens when the mother denies to herself that she is pregnant, despite the growing signs. When his wife's labour came, she was in a state of complete panic. It was as if she didn't know what was happening. She hadn't wanted to go to the hospital. She said she had the stomach flu.

"I blame myself," he said. "I blame myself for not really helping her."

Within a week of the birth, she had disappeared. She checked herself out of the hospital, and took the baby with her. It took him nine months to find the son — nine months of his son's life he knew nothing about. And then came the legal battles with the Children's Aid Society.

"What happened to her? What happened to your wife?"

"She committed suicide," he said quietly. "She was only nineteen."

That was all he could say.

He said he had known all along that Franny wasn't pregnant.

"How do you explain, then," Franny wanted to know, "the three-month absence of my period?"

"It was a false pregnancy. You wanted his baby. You still

love him and don't know it. That's why you're going back."

Franny felt her face burn. She wanted to hit him. "That's not true," she said. "It's a lie." She hit him in the chest.

"Is it?" he asked. "Is it?"

He took her roughly. He loved her in anger. He planted a hand on either side of her and caged her within his arms. He forced her legs apart with his knee. She felt something turn over in her, a deep excitement between her ribs.

"Don't forget me," he said, "don't forget you're coming back."

That night Franny had a dream. Her mother came to her by train. They met on a dark night, between cars. She held a box in her hands. Franny could not hear what her mother was trying to say to her. The squeal of metal drowned out the words. Lights flashed across her face. Her face was full of a mother's love and something else—a strange new fear. They did not kiss or embrace. Their meeting was coldly unemotional. She had come all that way and Franny did not even kiss her. Her mother placed the box in her hands and sadly withdrew. Franny knew that in the box was her unborn baby.

On the last night, he took her to a Portuguese restaurant. It was called *le fado*. He told her that a *fado* is a sad song a sailor sings for his country, missing his home.

"You made my summer," he told her. "I know this hasn't been a very good summer for you."

He was sitting back in his chair, a little distant from her. His arms were folded across his chest. His body looked

[35]

relaxed. The body of her lover. Strong and quiet. He was letting her go.

He told her of a dream he had had the other night. It was the first time he had ever dreamt of her, he said, a sign that in a way she had already left.

In his dream, a tree was burning in the corner of the living room. It was burning from inside. He could see this through a fissure in its bark. He took a sheet from his bed and began to wrap it around the trunk, thinking to smother the flames. But as he bound the tree, he felt the heat grow fiercer. He had to unwind the sheet to take a second look. Through the crack, he saw flames turning the whole inside to white ash. It must have been burning like that for the longest time. He realized he would have to take an axe and cut through to where it burned, to put it out from inside. But how could he, without felling the whole tree? He had understood, then, he could do nothing for the tree.

"I woke knowing the fire was your love for him, and that you, somehow, were the tree."

He took Franny's hand. He turned it over and laid a kiss in the palm. He looked down at the palm and touched it with his fingers, as if to see if his kiss had left any impression.

"You don't have a lifeline," he remarked unexpectedly, and looked up at her in surprise.

"That's ridiculous," she said, "I'm here aren't I?"

But something in this palm business had made her think about the way they met. They had been waiting for a bus. He had a cup of coffee in one hand, and took practised sips from a hole he had poked through the lid. He looked very relaxed, newspaper tucked comfortably under an arm. She was furious at having just missed the bus, at the prospect of the wait. He watched her pacing with humour. "You're from out of town," he said, finally. "After living on the coast for a while, you'll develop webbed feet. You won't take waiting so seriously." She had pulled the newspaper from under his arm and began flipping, transferring her impatience to its pages. "Would you mind telling me where to find the horoscopes in this paper?" "In the comic section," he told her. "Doesn't that undermine their credibility?"

"That's ridiculous," she said. "I'm here aren't I?"

"Are you, Franny? Were you ever here? Sometimes your love felt like something I intercepted."

Franny looked away. She felt ashamed. She had needed him to love her. She felt responsible for this.

"Once," she began, "I sat in on one of his math classes. He taught at the university. I wanted to surprise him, to watch him at his work. For a whole hour we were in the same room together, without his ever once seeing me. When the class was over, I went up to him. I stood among the students near his desk. He looked right at me, without seeing me, as if I weren't there. Did it happen, I wonder? Or was it just something I imagined? It made my whole life seem tenuous."

He shifted in his seat. He would be imagining her there. He would see her face waiting to surprise another man. The thought of it would pain him.

"When I left him, he never called me. Not even once. Not even to ask why it happened. It was as if we had never been

married. I lied to you about that, about seeing him before I
left. I didn't have to run away. He would never have come
after me.... Don't hate me," she said, finally. "I have to go
home."

Silence. His low voice. "I know," he said. "I know, Franny."

"I just wanted you to know."

They agreed not to have any train-station parting. They
agreed not to write. "There must be some reality to our relationship," he said. But she was tasting prairie dust when she
wrote her first letter, and there was a letter waiting for her
when she got home:

> It has been two days since I saw you and it seems as if you
> are just around the corner somewhere, but I just haven't
> stumbled around that right corner yet. It's a feeling of help-
> lessness. You were here, and then gone, and nothing is the
> same since you left. Today, one type of event: riding on the
> bus down Hastings past your old stop. There was a girl walk-
> ing. Slender, she was, with long hair swinging down her back.
> It embarrasses me to say that my heart skipped a beat. I
> almost choked. Back to my senses before the bus passed her, I
> strained to see her face. (She did not even look like you.) And
> when *will* I see you again? For I must see you again, Franny,
> impossible as it seems. These last two days have been of
> unprecedented duration. How will I bear the wait?

The letters that followed were always constant in their tone. They were even, and tender, and wise. A new voice had emerged in them. It spoke of things with wry humour. Whenever Franny read his letters, she thought of his laugh, the way he had laughed with his chin tucked into his chest.

They were two years into writing letters when he said he was coming east. He would be whatever she wanted, he said. He would be lover, or husband, or friend. She had only to say the word.

But Franny was afraid of the changes that had taken place in her. She knew she had left the West for a reason, though that reason might be long divorced from her. She was afraid of bringing him all that way for nothing. She wrote and asked him not to come.

A year went by without a letter. When she wrote again, it was a few words on a Christmas card. The letter that followed was a long sigh of relief. With what joy she found it in the mail slot, returning to her apartment after a brief holiday. "He has forgiven me," she thought. It was as if there had never been any break. In the letter, he spoke of a journey he had made with his son. They had "cruised across country," he said, in one of the wide-tracking Pontiacs he was "wheeling about with these days." He had taken his son to see the hospital where he was born. Franny understood then that her lover was making peace with his past. He had gone back for reasons not unconnected with the ones that impelled her home.

His dream proved prophetic. Franny burned from inside. She burned like that for the longest time, and there was nothing he could have done for her. She thought it strange at the time that a man could love a woman who bore the signs of another upon her skin. But the time would eventually come when the burning would stop, all on its own. And then she would write, and ask him to come.

the question

*"When I burned in desire to question them further, they made themselves
into air, into which they vanished."*

—LADY MACBETH

I WAS A young woman then—single and without child—
green in the practice of my profession, when I had this
dream: A great litigator gave me a powerful secret—the one
question that, when asked, would unlock all the secrets of
another's soul, heave truth to lip, would compel any witness
to tell everything. There is a cardinal rule among litigators
that is hard to reconcile with the purpose of the question in
my dream: never ask a question in cross-examination for
which the answer is unknown. A litigator must never let a
personal curiosity impair his control of the case. The
unknown answer is dangerous and unpredictable. In the art of
cross-examination, it is the questions that matter more than
the answers.

The Toronto apartment building where Edna Hamilton lived
was old and dingy. As we climbed the stairs to Edna
Hamilton's apartment, my winded boss said how he hated

"these airless hallways." His secretary had told me to meet him down at the YMCA at 8:00 o'clock in the morning after his exercise class. He had a file for me that "wanted a woman lawyer." We went to a door, knocked, and an old woman answered. She could have been anyone's grandmother.

There was no air conditioning, and although it was early morning, Edna Hamilton already had the venetian blinds closed and the burgundy and green floral curtains drawn across the blinds to keep out the summer's heat. Everything was meticulously neat, exactly what one would expect of an old woman's apartment. It was as if Edna Hamilton had moved in thirty years ago when the building was new and everything within her four walls had stayed still, while the building had run down around her.

My boss reviewed the statement of claim with which Edna Hamilton had been served.

She was being sued by a dead man's estate for the return of some $82,000, plus interest. The claim alleged that the money had belonged to Frank Duvaliers, Edna's dead brother-in-law. The executor was one of the many sons the dead man had collected through his many marriages. The executor wanted this money back for the benefit of the dead man's heirs, of which he was one, of course.

"The money wasn't Frank's. Frank never had two nickels to scratch. It was Jeannette Bell's, my dead sister's child. She gave it to me seven years ago — to keep it out of her father's clutches, no doubt."

"Do you have the cancelled cheque?" my boss asked the old woman.

Edna produced a copy of a cheque she had obtained from the Jefferson Bank, Louisiana. It was dated seven years earlier, was in the amount of $82,672.35, and clearly stated that it was to the order of our client by the remitter, Jeannette Bell.

"There's your defence," the great litigator told me. "Gift from the niece. Never Frank's money. Estate has no greater claim to it than Frank would, if alive. You draft the defence," he said to me before he left. "Make sure you get the whole story."

Throughout the balance of that day, I listened to what I thought was Edna's story:

"He murdered my sister. Over my dead body will any of that crowd get one cent. Dead or alive, he was nothing but trouble....

"She was eighteen when she married him. We lived on the same street, in Perth, Ontario. Thick as thieves, we were, my sister and I. Jeannette was her first. There was a baby every year after that. I was pregnant myself when Frank brought me the news. 'If you ever want to see your sister alive again,' he says, 'come with me now.' I didn't know what he was talking about. I grabbed my coat. I had to run to keep up with him as we climbed the hill to the hospital. Then I saw her. A tube from every hole. Just the day before, she'd opened her front door to me, a baby on her hip. She dropped the diaper she held and we both went down to pick it up together. She smelled of milk and powder, my sister. I remember it like yesterday. A mother with three babes, and yet a babe herself. There was still breast milk on some of the blouses I washed after the funeral. That wasn't her in that hospital bed — hair pasted to her face, eyes sunken in like she was already dead. 'Bring me my babies,' she says to me, 'one at a time.' I had time just to kiss her, no time to ask a question. I ran down the hill to the house again. I called for Jeannette to hurry now quickly and put on her coat. Jeannette was just over three.

"Jeannette came running to her at first, but when she saw the hand, she drew back. It had a needle taped to it. 'It's all right,' my sister says to Jeannette, 'Mommy's just going to sleep now,' and for the longest time, it seemed as it she had just gone to sleep. I had to take Jeannette away, finally. Just as we were leaving the room, my sister spoke to me again. 'Take care of my babies.' Those were the last words she ever spoke. She died while I was bringing her boy up the hill.

"'I never knew it would kill her,' was all Frank Duvaliers ever had to say about it. That was years later. Thirty years, when I finally caught up with him. He took off the day after the funeral. He took off with my sister's kids. I paid for the funeral. I paid for her plot. I paid for the rent that was over-due on their ramshackle of a house. I washed and ironed and sold or gave away my dead sister's clothes. I paid for the debts Frank Duvaliers left behind. He got away with murder, he did. Because that's what it was. She was only twenty-one at the time."

There was a long bitter silence. Then I asked, "Why did he leave?"

"Why do you think?" Edna blinked at me through indignant eyes, as if to say, how could I be a lawyer and woman, yet not know this?

"Abortion was illegal at the time. The hospital knew what

had been done. The police were probably just waiting till after she'd been buried."

"How did you find him?"

"Now there's a story. New Orleans. Thirty years later, I had time to kill between bus connections. I was looking through the phone book. I used to look for his name whenever I went to a strange city. Sure enough, there it was. I called the number. Frank was curious enough to invite me over. He had them all over at the house by the time I got there. Of course, they weren't babies anymore.

"They all wanted to hear about their mother. Frank had told them she died in childbirth. But Jeannette couldn't remember any baby. Wouldn't she have at least seen the baby? She was sharp as nails, that one. She even remembered asking at the graveside, 'What happens when she wakes up? How will she get out?' She remembered the question, but not what anyone answered. Can you imagine asking such a thing? She even remembered the hospital and the trip up the hill. She told me she had cried the first time it rained. 'That made two of us,' I said, but by then, they'd have been somewhere in the eastern United States. It must have rained a different day.

"We were doing dishes in Frank's kitchen, me and Jeannette, when I told her the truth. Just then Frank came in the kitchen. 'I didn't think it would kill her,' he says. And I knew then for sure what I'd only suspected for years."

"What did you do?"

"What do you mean, what did I do?"

"Well, did you confront him?"

"We finished the dishes. Me and Jeannette."

But what about the lives in between, the lives of the babes over which Edna was to have taken such care? Had been charged to do so by her dying sister? A deathbed request.

At fifteen, Jeannette's father made her strip in the bathroom and beat her with his belt until she passed out. Frank stopped, thinking he had killed her. The beating caused the injury that caused the plastic-vein replacement operation that ultimately killed Jeannette in later years.

Jeannette's brother ran away from home at fourteen and worked on a farm until Frank found him and pulled him back. He left again at the legal age of sixteen.

"The boy is dead now, too," Edna tells me, "committed suicide at sixty. They found him swinging from the rafters of the barn Jeannette helped him buy."

For Jeannette made a financial success of her life—buying convenience store operations, trading in real estate. "She was sharp as nails, that one."

And then there were Frank's marriages: After Edna's sister, Frank married a diabetic widow with three children of her own, who in the end wouldn't trust Frank to give her the insulin needle. When Frank's second wife died, Frank married her sister, who also happened to be his dead brother's wife, becoming father to more stepchildren. They all called him "uncle."

"Imagine marrying your brother's wife, your wife's sister? It's like incest. There wasn't a crime Frank Duvaliers didn't commit."

Thirty years of catch-up. Another twenty go by. And in the twenty, Edna takes the place of Jeannette's mother.

Jeannette visits Edna in Canada, and Edna comes south. Jeannette sends Mother's Day cards on Mother's Day, becoming more of a daughter to Edna than Edna's own.

Jeannette is fifty-three years of age and Edna over seventy when Jeannette sends the certified cheque to Canada in the amount of $82,672.35, drawn on the Jefferson Bank. No letter. No explanation. Just the cheque. Edna goes across the hallway and shows it to a neighbour. "Do you think it's real?" Then she telephones Jeannette.

"Do what you want with it," Jeannette tells her. "Invest it, buy a house — it's yours."

A few months later, Jeannette goes into hospital for routine surgery on her leg to have the plastic vein replaced. She dies of a hemorrhage on the operating table.

And now Frank's heirs are suing for the money. They say it was Frank's — all because of a receipt found in Frank Duvaliers's safe after his death.

"How did Frank come by the receipt?"

"He stole it," Edna tells me without hesitation. "He stole it from Jeannette. He was always stealing from his rich daughter."

"But why a receipt?"

"How should I know how Frank's mind worked? The foolish man probably thought to take some action on it during his life," she tells me.

"Where is the money now?"

Edna sits in her chair, her hands neatly folded in her lap. She gives me a level stare, looking amazingly pink and determined for someone over eighty.

"It's gone. As far as Frank Duvaliers and his crowd are concerned, there isn't a cent of it left. I'll fight this until there isn't a cent. He murdered my sister. He should have hung fifty years ago."

I am thrilled by the story, buoyed up by it all day. I return to the office in a froth of indignation—that anyone could sue Edna Hamilton after all these years, after all she has been through. My boss listens to me speak with that Cheshire smile he wears on his face for a case well matched to its counsel, and then asks the simple question that stops me in my tracks:

"You believe her?"

"Of course I do. Don't you?"

"Take some advice: Never believe what your own client tells you. That way, you may be pleasantly surprised, but you'll never be disappointed."

But the case is mine. I write an outraged letter to opposing counsel and tell him that if the estate of Frank Duvaliers goes away now, we'll let them off lightly; pursue this spurious litigation, we'll be looking for costs. Opposing counsel writes back demanding dates for the discovery. He encloses documents. Among the estate's documents are two inexplicable letters:

Dear Jeannette and Frank,

Here it is 3 p.m. & I've just gotten home from the Bank.

Jeannette, I have good news for you, the interest rate went up a per cent today so you are getting 15½ % interest on your money. I can't understand your Dad. If left in the Jefferson Bank, the money would only have lain there at about 9% at most. I think you are better off with it here. You could have had it in your name if you had sent the money directly from the Jefferson Bank to my Bank here, but you would have had to pay American income tax and also the Bank would have had to deduct 15% of the interest in instalments for the Canadian withholding tax because you live outside Canada and are drawing interest from Canadian sources. I will explain it better when I come down.

If your Dad wants to drop in, tell him by all means to come. I am alone and he has no need to worry about Mr. Hamilton. I am still classed as "single" and I don't care who he lives with or if he goes through a form of marriage. He can have a harem, if he is man enough.

Aunt Edna

Dear Jeannette,

Just a hasty note asking you to send back to me the receipt I sent you. I must have it to return to the bank at the end of the term deposit. It is wise you have no papers where Frank's money has gone. Also, destroy any bank numbers regarding the book. It is only good to me, seeing it has my name only on any transactions. If these people are bent on trouble, there's no use giving them any opportunity to find out where Frank's money went. It is Frank's money. I will not give any part to anyone, only Frank, at the end of five years. He trusted this amount to me and I will honour that trust to the end.

Did not see my granddaughter. It was a strange thing for her to phone me, seeing I did not know her and really have no desire to be involved with any of these people. I have gotten along all these years without them. Now out of the blue they appear on the horizon. My desire for all my grandchildren is for them to retire back into the sunset and continue to forget me, as have their parents.

Tell your Dad to drop in when he comes to Canada.

Aunt Edna

The day before the scheduled examinations, I go again to Edna's apartment to prepare her for discovery. I show her the letters. Edna sits in her chair and reads them silently. After she has finished reading them, she looks at me calmly. Her eyes above the line that separates her bifocals are small and sharp, below the line, swollen and unfocused, like two blobs of runny jelly.

These letters, I tell her, are a problem.

You think they are a problem?

Clearly, I tell her. For example, what did you mean by "Frank's money"? Why are you accounting to Frank and Jeannette for the interest rate? Why did you send Jeannette a receipt? What's all this concern about tax implications of the transfer if the money was a gift? I rattle off a whole series of questions relevant to the lawsuit, and then I tell Edna these are the kinds of questions she will be asked on the morrow. But in my mind, there is another question that I have no excuse for asking. Why did you invite Frank to come to you? Your sister's murderer....

… I am alone… I am still single…

"Do you know what I think?" Edna tells me that day. "I think Frank stole the money from his second wife. He was involved in litigation for years, you know, with her kids. They finally got a court order to kick him out of her house. But when they went looking for her money, it was gone."

Only afterwards do I realize I left that day without any answers. But my questions accomplished what they were meant to accomplish professionally: They prepared Edna Hamilton for discovery.

THE DISCOVERIES

Q. Mrs. Hamilton, I am showing you a letter dated May 12, 1981. It is addressed to "Dear Jeannette and Frank." Can you identify this, please, as your letter?

A. I have no recollection of writing this letter.

Q. Could you take a moment to look at the handwriting and tell me whether or not you recognize it as your own handwriting?

A. I have no recollection of writing this at all. I am sorry.

Q. I am not asking you whether you recollect writing it. My question to you is, do you recognize the handwriting?

A. The handwriting can't be mine if I can't recollect writing it.

Q. Do you deny that this is your handwriting?

A. I have no recollection of writing this.

Q. I can write a letter and not remember writing it, but that does not mean it is not my writing. I am asking you if that is your handwriting.

A. I don't think so.

Q. Are you not sure?

A. I have no idea of ever writing it, so therefore I couldn't have written it.

Q. Mrs. Hamilton, I am going to show you another document. Is that in your handwriting?

A. I can't honestly say.

Q. You neither deny nor confirm it?

[Me] You have her answer, she cannot honestly say. She cannot identify it one way or the other as her handwriting.

Q. Okay. Well, then, I will have to live with that for now.

But I cannot live with it. I could not live with it then. I cannot live with it now.

★ ★ ★

Q. Mrs. Hamilton, do you recall telling Jeannette that if her father wanted to drop in and visit that by all means he was welcome to do that?

A. No.

Q. Did Frank Duvaliers visit you in 1981?

A. No, he did not.

Q. Did Frank Duvaliers ever visit you for the purpose of collecting money?

A. No.

Q. He never did?

   A. Never.

[*Me*] Did he ever visit you?

   A. No, never.

★ ★ ★

   Q. Were you provided with some sort of paper from the bank at the time you bought the term deposit to show that you had a term deposit with the bank?

   A. You mean a receipt?

   Q. Yes. Were you given a receipt?

   A. Yes.

   Q. And do you have that here with you today?

   A. No.

   Q. What became of that?

   A. I sent it to Jeannette.

   Q. Yes?

   A. And that was the last I saw of it.

   Q. Why would you send a receipt to Jeannette?

   A. Just to show her what I had done with the money, that's all. No purpose other than that.

   Q. Did you, sometime before the term deposit matured, attempt to recover from Jeannette the receipt you had sent her?

   A. I asked her for it, yes, on the phone.

   Q. Did you also send her a letter asking for it?

   A. I don't remember sending her a letter. I phoned her all the time.

   Q. Why did you want the return of the receipt?

   A. Well, a receipt's a receipt, isn't it? No particular reason.

[53]

Q. When the term deposit matured, did you not need that receipt?

A. No, I went to the bank and they gave me another one, but I can't tell you where that is either.

Q. Why would you find it necessary to send Jeannette the receipt when you had already told her on the phone what you had done with the money?

A. Well, just to, I mean, she was like a daughter to me. We didn't keep any secrets or anything from each other. She was actually like my daughter. Her mother was my sister.

[Me] Counsel, you might want to ask what reason Jeannette gave for not sending the receipt back to Edna Hamilton.

[DISCUSSION OFF THE RECORD]

Q. Do you recall, Mrs. Hamilton, being visited or attempted to be visited by a granddaughter?

A. No. Granddaughter of whom? My own?

Q. Yes. Do you have grandchildren?

A. I have grandchildren, I don't see them.

Q. How many grandchildren do you have?

A. I would imagine ten or twelve.

Q. And you don't see any of them?

A. No. In fact, I haven't seen them, not even when they were born. I have never seen them. You may find it odd, but it's true.

Q. Yes, it is strange.

A. It is strange, but—

Q. Would you like to see them?

A. No. I have no desire, not now. They're grown up and married.

★ ★ ★

Q. You are aware that Frank Duvaliers remarried again, subsequent to May of 1981, a person by the name of Margaret Duvaliers.

A. Yes.

Q. And Margaret Duvaliers, she has been previously married to Frank's brother, is that true?

A. That's right. I don't know her, mind you.

Q. And Frank had previously been married to her sister?

A. Yes.

Q. Do you deny that she, subsequent to being married to Frank, in about 1981 or 1982, visited you here in Toronto?

A. Visited me?

Q. Yes.

A. I've never seen the lady. I don't know her, never set eyes on her, never in my life.

[*Me*] Let the record reflect my client's surprise.

A. I have never seen her. She was the third wife, you know. The second wife was her sister. And the third wife was married to Frank's brother before Frank. They're all dead now. Everybody's dead. Except me. [Laughter] Aren't I awful?

★ ★ ★

Q. Is there any reason you know of why Jeannette would give this money to you by way of a gift?

A. I told you, she was like a daughter to me.

Q. And for what period of time had you carried on a relationship with Jeannette that she was like a daughter?

A. About twenty years.

Q. Had she ever given you money before?

A. No.

Q. And did she ever subsequently?

A. No.

Q. Had she ever given you anything else, anything other than money?

A. No, just...you know, cards, Christmas cards, birthday cards, things such as that. She never missed an occasion for cards. I have two or three albums here full of them if you want to see.

Q. I would, yes, actually, if your counsel doesn't mind.

[Me] Go ahead.

★ ★ ★

Q. Did you have any conversation with Frank Duvaliers after receiving these funds?

A. No.

Q. Any conversation at all?

A. No.

Q. Either by phone, any correspondence, or contact?

A. No.

Q. None?

A. None.

Q. Mrs. Hamilton, you have indicated in your Statement of Defence that there is a family history here that might have bearing on the issues, arising out of the fact that Frank was married to your sister. Your sister died?

A. Yes.

Q. What did your sister die of?

A. An illegal abortion.

Q. An illegal abortion?

A. Yes.

Q. Did she not undergo an abortion in the hospital?

A. No. Wasn't allowed then, young man.

Q. Do you have any knowledge of where it was that she underwent an abortion?

A. At home.

Q. And where was that at the time?

A. Northern Ontario.

Q. And how do you know that?

A. I lived there.

Q. You lived with them?

A. No, I lived with my husband up the street.

Q. And were you present during the abortion?

A. No, I saw her in the hospital afterward.

Q. And do you know who performed the illegal abortion?

A. Yes.

Q. Who?

A. Frank Duvaliers.

Q. How do you know that?

A. He told me himself.

Q. He told you himself?

A. Yes.

Q. Now, you have got here that your sister had asked you to take care of her children?

A. Yes.

Q. Do you have any indication that Frank was not prepared to take care of his own children at the time?

A. I don't know. My sister asked me if I'd go down and look after her babies. He took them off to Mexico, to the States, to Mexico.

Q. Did you ever report Frank Duvaliers to any authorities?

A. No, because at the time I didn't know that he was the one who did the abortion.

★ ★ ★

Q. Now, in your defence, you say, "It was generally known by the family that Jeannette had given this money to the Defendant." What family are you referring to?

A. Jeannette's.

Q. You are referring to her two children?

A. I think they all knew. I would imagine they would know.

Q. What evidence do you have that it was generally known?

A. Well, I would imagine they did a lot of talking. I don't know. I wasn't there.

★ ★ ★

Q. Did you touch any part of the principal monies before the maturity date on the term deposit?

A. No.

Q. What did you do with the interest earned on the term deposit?

A. Spent it.

Q. You spent all of it?

A. Yes.

Q. Pardon me?

A. Yes.

Q. What did you do with the principal after the term deposit matured?

A. Spent it.

Q. You spent it?

A. Yes. It was *given to me*, you know. I didn't steal that money. Understand that, young man?

Q. How did you spend it?

A. Good heavens, I couldn't tell you every place I spent it.

Q. Have you made any gifts to anybody since the beginning of this legal proceeding?

A. I really don't think that is any of your concern. I can do what I like with my money, you know.

Q. Is any of the principal or interest left on the money you say was given to you by Jeannette?

A. Not one cent.

[RE-EXAMINATION]

[*Me*] You recall being asked about a receipt. What was the reason Jeannette gave you for not having the receipt available to send back to you?

    A. Her father had it. He stole it out of her papers.

    Q. Thank you. No further questions.

[*Counsel*] Let the record show that during the period of time we were off the record, counsel had the opportunity to refresh her witness on that very evidence.

   [*Me*] No, let the record reflect that while off the record, I indicated to counsel that there might be a question he would want to ask, and when he asked the question and got the same response I have just obtained from my client, he said he did not want it on the record and I told him I would ask that question in reply.

[*Counsel*] We can argue this until the cows come home.

   [*Me*] In any event, I will have my opportunity to examine Mrs. Hamilton in chief and *we will get the whole story at the trial.*

Frank's funeral must have been an animated event. It took place in Moncton, New Brunswick. After the burial, everyone returned to the house that had belonged to his third wife before her death. Those present included the sole surviving daughter of his first marriage and the children of Frank's second and third wives. Walter, son of the third wife and executor of Frank's estate, was also there. Imagine everyone's excitement when he went down into the basement and opened the safe. There was a shoebox inside. In the shoebox he found the letters. Upstairs, around the table, Walter read the letters aloud to the assembly. Walter took them to a lawyer the very next day. They all wanted to see what should be done about it. They all figured it was Frank's money; it should be put back. They all wanted their fair share, this greedy little bunch.

Now it is my turn to question Frank's executor, the representative of this estate:

Q. You'll agree with me, sir, that the Last Will and Testament of Frank Duvaliers appears to have been made some three years after the gift of money to Edna Hamilton.

A. Yes.

Q. Now, I note from the will that Frank was quite specific as to bequeathing certain things. For instance, his tools.

A. Yes.

Q. And he has also bequeathed a gold watch and ring to a great grandson.

A. Yes.

Q. And a truck to someone else.

A. Yes.

Q. Now, from the Statement of Receipts and Disbursements, you'll agree with me that the total funds in the estate appear to be about $114,000.

A. Yes.

Q. And you'll agree with me that nowhere in the will is there mentioned a sum of approximately $80,000 United States dollars, which Frank believed he had as part of his property.

A. No, it wasn't mentioned in the will.

Q. Don't you think that was odd?

A. Well, a little bit, yes.

Q. Why does that strike you as odd, sir, now upon reflection? Is it because it's a large sum of money?

A. Yes, right.

Q. Relative to what was in his estate at the time of his death?

A. Yes.

Q. In fact, it's larger than the sum of money that was available at the time of his death. You'll agree with me?

A. Larger?

Q. Yes, $80,000 U.S. funds at the time he allegedly sent it to Edna Hamilton would be worth a lot more seven years later at the time of his death.

A. Yes.

Q. And yet no mention of it at all in the will.

A. No.

Q. Now, I'm told that at the time Frank married your mother, your mother had cancer and was, in fact, dying.

A. Not to my knowledge.

Q. But she died, in fact, within a year of the marriage.

A. Yes, that's correct.

Q. What did you think of him?

A. Who, of Frank? You mean personally? I found him a real nice man.

Q. So, you approved of his marriage to your mother?

A. Yes.

Q. Did you trust him?

A. Yes.

Q. Did you generally find him a trustworthy person?

A. Yes.

Q. Did you think he was a rich man?

A. No.

Q. Did you think he was a man of means?

A. I never really thought about it.

Q. Did you assume he had enough money to support your mother?

A. Well, my mother could have supported herself.

Q. At your mother's funeral, did you ever say to Frank Duvaliers, "Where's my mother's money?" or words to that effect?

A. No, I never said that. I didn't care.

Q. Did your mother have an estate?

A. Yes.

Q. What did that consist of?

A. Her home and her car.

Q. What about bank deposits?

A. As far as I know, she and Frank had joint bank accounts. All the money went to Frank.

Q. You never said to him, "What became of my Mom's money?"

A. No.

Q. Is it true that your family — you and your brothers and sisters — made Frank sign his pension over to your mother at the time of their marriage?

A. No.

Q. So you deny that.

A. Yes.

Q. In fact, the children of Frank's third wife did quite well by Frank's will.

A. Not really, because a lot of that money was my mother's.

Q. When you say a lot of the money was your mother's, what percentage would you have in mind?

A. I'm not really sure, but when Frank came to Canada, he didn't have that much.

Q. How much did he bring?

A. About $11,000.

Q. $11,000. So, if we've got about $100,000 in bank deposits at the time of his death, only about 10% of that would have been his. The rest was your mother's? Is that a fair statement?

A. Yes.

Q. So, this is a man who comes to Moncton with about $11,000 to his name. And a few years later he's making a will. And according to your theory of the case, he believes that there's a woman holding $80,000 U.S. of monies that belong to him. And he doesn't say a thing about it in his will. Would you agree with me that's a pretty significant omission?

[*Counsel*] I object to that. It's not omitted from the will. Specific reference is not made, but it's not omitted and that is a question of law, which my client is not going to answer.

Q. Do you have any explanation, sir, for Frank's delay — no, it's more than delay — for his *failure* to ever institute legal proceedings to get this money back during his lifetime, during his remaining seven years?

A. No, I don't.

Q. No explanation whatsoever?

A. No.

Q. Let me put this proposition to you: If those monies were dirty monies, if those monies were stolen, or if those monies would have attracted a criminal charge if the late Frank Duvaliers instituted proceedings to get them back, is there any reason why the estate should be able to prosecute this action with impunity?

[*Counsel*] That calls for speculation on the part of my client, and I refuse to let him answer that question.

Q. I would like to know why Frank Duvaliers did not institute proceedings for this money during this lifetime.

A. The man to answer that question is not here on the earth today.

Q. The man to answer that question is not here on earth, but he apparently has quite a number of spokespersons, judging by the number of people talking after his funeral.

[*Counsel*] We'll undertake to provide you with any information we can obtain as to whether the monies were dirty monies. This is the first we've heard of it.

[*Me*] Well, no, the first you heard of it was from your own client's mouth—that he was told by Jeannette's sister that Frank was worried about criminal charges.

A. No, I didn't say that. Edna told him that. Jeannette's sister told me that when Frank came to get the money from Edna, Edna threatened him that she would lay charges against him for smuggling his money or taking it out of the States or something.

Q. The fact remains, sir, that for seven years, to the best of your knowledge, no steps whatsoever of a legal nature were taken by Frank to obtain the return of those monies.

A. Not that I know of.

Q. And you think you can come to court behind the smokescreen of an estate, where Frank couldn't come in his lifetime?

[*Counsel*] Don't answer that.

Q. I have information that there was a bank passbook of Frank's second wife among the papers in Frank's shoebox, and that passbook unlocked the mystery that had been tormenting her kids for years and which was probative of the sum of $80,000 having been, in effect, stolen from his second wife's bank account prior to her death. This bank passbook of the second wife shows the withdrawal of $80,000 just prior to her death in hospital. Did such a passbook, to your knowledge, show up in the shoebox?

A. Not to my knowledge.

Q. Now, there is a statement that is attributed to Frank's only surviving daughter of his first marriage regarding the tone after the funeral of Frank Duvaliers—and I quote this roughly: "You should have seen them all arguing like cats and dogs." Would you describe the tone following Frank's funeral as analogous to the arguments of cats and dogs?

A. That's all news to me. I couldn't have been there. I must have been asleep.

Q. How would you describe the tone after the funeral?

A. No different than after any funeral—everybody just sitting around the table talking and drinking tea.

Q. So, there was no dismay about the will? There were no hard feelings?

A. Well, I wouldn't say no hard feelings. Somebody's *always* bound to be *disappointed*.

★ ★ ★

Q. You indicated that your wife received the will from Frank at the time she took him to hospital.

A. Yes.

Q. When he gave it to her, did he tell her that, in addition to this will, there's also the money Edna Hamilton is holding for him?

A. I don't think he did, because I never heard her mention anything like that.

Q. Did he ever, in the time he was in hospital—how long was he in hospital?

A. Three or four days.

Q. Did he, at any time he was in hospital, mention Edna Hamilton?

A. Not to my knowledge.

★ ★ ★

Q. You indicated that there were some photographs that you came across when you went through the papers. Is that right?

A. Yes.

Q. Were any of those photographs of Edna Hamilton?

A. No.

Q. Or Frank Duvaliers?

A. No.

Q. If you come across any photographs of Edna Hamilton, will you produce them for me?

A. Yes.

[*Counsel*] How is this relevant?

As if a picture could tell: Who was Edna Hamilton? Who was Frank Duvaliers? What power did he have over women? Such a power that his first wife had not accused him of her death. Was she like that lady in the newspaper I read about, so in love with her murderer that when her own dying daughter asked her, "Why did you let him do it, Momma, why did you let him douse us in kerosene and light a match?" she answered, "I don't think he knew it was kerosene." Such a power that a dying woman signed a cheque to Frank Duvaliers in preference to her own flesh and blood? Such a power that the dead woman's sister took him in when her sister's children got a court order kicking him out of her dead sister's house? Such a power that the daughter he had stripped and beaten in a bathroom at the age of fifteen helped him get the money out of Jefferson, away from people "bent on making trouble"? Such a power that Edna invited him, her sister's murderer, to herself: "… *tell him by all means to come. I am alone and he has no need to worry about Mr. Hamilton. I am still classed as 'single'…*"

Why had Edna Hamilton not reported Frank Duvaliers to the authorities? Why had she searched for him for thirty years? Why had she written those words in her letter—"I am alone...I am single..."—words meant for a man she believed had murdered her sister? Was it love? Was it hate? Was it revenge? Was it anything one question could illuminate?

Here's what I think must have happened: Edna Hamilton did not take Frank's money. It wasn't Frank's money. It wasn't Jeannette's. It was the money of the dead second wife. Edna was right about that. Because she knew Frank. She knew how Frank lived off women. He'd got his sickly diabetic wife, the wife who didn't trust him to give her the insulin needle in the end, to sign a cheque to him while in hospital. He had to get the money out of Jefferson, using the only people he could trust. He sent it to Edna, using Jeannette. *He sent it to Edna. Edna was someone he could trust.* How did he know that? Why did he think he could trust Edna Hamilton? Why did Edna take the money? Why did she write Jeannette, "tell him by all means to come"?

★ ★ ★

The afternoon after her sister's death, Edna went to meet him. No one ever knew. She went to him to ask him a question, but all the way there, all the way to that ramshackle of a rented house her dead sister had scrubbed and curtained and filled with the smells of babies and milk, all she could think of was the two of them, Frank and her sister, how they had looked at each other their first summer in love, what their love had done to her, how it had tormented her in bed at night through a whole summer of restlessness, uncovered on the creased sheets, tossing for loneliness until the sound of geese going south released her, a season dead, the earth cooling and only beginning to hunger. She married Mr. Hamilton the next spring.

Edna is sitting on the couch; Frank is at the window. It is the first day after her sister's death. Frank pauses with his hand holding back the curtain, watching something in the street. His lengthy body, with its thick thighs and low sex, weight poised on one hip, arms crossed on his sloping chest with the sleeves rolled up; his presence, so physical, with its unaroused sensuality. They are both young. He pours them a drink. Edna is three months pregnant and knows she shouldn't take it. But she does. As he hands the glass to her, their hands touch.

He stands with one hand in the pocket of his pleated pants, his face in profile as he stares out the window at something in the street. Suddenly, he tugs on the chord of the venetian blinds, sending them crashing. For no reason at all, Edna gives Frank a memory. It isn't even real:

"When I was a little girl, I used to image this dark man who'd come to the house while my father was at work. I'd feel him in the house like a shadow — someone who had always just gone, who had waited for me, who I always missed by staying out a minute longer."

"Was there?"

"Was there what?"

"A man."

"No, … I don't think so."

Frank stares now at the floor as if he can see through it, or is listening intently to something in the next room. Edna listens too. They hear only the kitchen clock. A neighbour is taking care of the kids.

"I don't know what I'm talking about." (She sounds drunk.)

"There's a lot you don't know."

"Look, I didn't come here to —"

"Why did you come?"

"Because my sister is dead."

Frank laughs. She listens to his laugh, the sharp cynicism of it driving furrows through the silence, turning her words over like clods of freshly exposed earth.

"You came because you're guilty."

"Why should *I* feel guilty? What did I have to do with this?"

"You tell me."

Edna has risen, looks around the room for her coat. The suddenness of her rising throws her off balance.

Frank puts his hands on her shoulders and pushes her back into her seat.

"Sit down, for Christ's sake. Besides, you don't want to go yet, and I don't want to be alone."

Edna accepts his hands on her shoulders, feels herself grow pink.

"What did you do to my sister, Frank?"

All of a sudden, the risk she has taken in coming occurs to her, makes her want to vomit. Trapped by this dark front room with its empty traces of her sister still lying about, by the possibility of Frank's violence, by his maleness.

As if he knows why she's frightened, Frank automatically

softens. He puts down his glass, and when he looks at her again, the expression in his eyes is completely different, gentler, reassuring, as if he wants her to stay, as if the moment before hasn't happened. She can't believe it.

"Why don't you stay?"

"I can't…"

But she doesn't go. She rises again and stands in the middle of the room, staring at the slats of light in the covered window, waiting, her mind unsettled, as if to go now would leave everything unfinished, as if somehow this isn't enough.

"I feel, I don't know.…"

"I know, I feel the same."

For a moment they stand together, not talking.

"Oh God," he says.

Edna believes she can feel him trembling. The weight of his pain draws her to him.

And then the most unexpected thing begins to happen. Standing together in that room, the absurdity of their standing together, after what has happened, suddenly breaks in on them. Frank and Edna begin to laugh. Caught by each other, laughing almost to tears, avoiding eyes at first, and then the one bitter glance through each other that sobers them both.

The next instant exists in outline, like the cartoon of an inspiration that awaits only its execution. For a moment they face each other in silence. The alternative is boredom. The alternative is the years with Mr. Hamilton and five small children, and the long years that follow Hamilton's desertion, of working at three jobs around the clock just to feed and clothe them—the ungrateful kids who will grow up anyway, who will grow up on their own and leave her too, not knowing who Edna Hamilton was until it almost doesn't matter that she was ever their mother. The alternative is boredom. But Frank and Edna are not bored. They both know it.

She had known then. And wasn't horrified. Intrigued, rather, that such a thing could happen, might even still happen; so fascinated that, standing at the door, they are lost in possibility.

He might close the door again…. He might take her coat and sling it over the chair, and take her, not scooped under as you'd hold out an offering, but one arm wrapped over her legs, closing her in so that her whole body was turned and hidden from itself against him, moulded around each rhythmic movement of his body toward the bedroom; the first cold contact of sheets, his unfamiliar nakedness, undressed clumsily against her, mouth finding her breasts, her stomach, not leaving her a moment. Edna closing her eyes as he undressed her, and then seized by a sudden panic, struggling underneath him, wanting to hurt, to bite hard, unable to go with his fierce increase of pleasure, finding herself parted—Frank, groaning, lowering the whole force of his weight into her, thrusting up into her stomach. She rises and wraps her legs around his back, her mouth open over his shoulder, his arms curled under her back, hands tugging down on her shoulders; she curves like a cup under his frightening strokes coming down into her until they both reach what she has come for….

Running, running back up the hill, three months pregnant with Hamilton's child, running back to her own safe life. For this is Frank's power—not the body's seduction, not just that for the few years he was married to her sister, Edna had touched him over and over again without really touching, not just sex, the need for which would die eventually, which would have made such a moment, had it really happened, seem ridiculous in retrospect to one as intelligent as Edna, such a waste of time, but that he, Frank, *knew her.* How had he known he could trust her? He—not bound to Edna's fantasies, the dreams she summoned for herself, the tricks she pulled to get herself privately through the years—Frank showed her, in his eyes, what she was up to all along. He has prepared to be whatever she wanted. He is the knower, Frank Duvaliers, one of her kind—devastating the mask in one instant of mutual recognition. Who is this Frank Duvaliers? Who but herself, the mirror of her own possibility?

Until he brought another sister to Canada. Until he chose another sister as his third and last bride. Until she lost the power to self-deceive.

She had never forgiven him that. He ought to have hung fifty years ago.

"The money's safe with me. I will not give any part of it to no one. Only to Frank at the end of five years." Edna took the money because she knew that Frank would follow it to Canada, that eventually he would come. And he did come. He came to her en route to Moncton. Only he came with a bride, the sister of his dead second wife. It was that—not the murder of her own sister, not the beating of the sister's child, not anything but that—his choice of a different sister when *this time she was free,* that dissipated his power over her…. *I am alone…I am single.*

That must have been some moment when he asked for his money. When she told him he wasn't going to get any of it, not one red cent. And if he tried to make trouble for her, she'd make trouble for him. She'd report him to the authorities for trying to defraud Internal Revenue. So Edna Hamilton had settled for Frank's money. She had let Frank trust her and, in one way anyway, the trust had paid off.

Did any of it happen? Did it happen that way?

I thought I would get the whole story at trial. But there never was a trial. The out-of-province estate failed to post security for Edna Hamilton's costs, and the claim was struck out against her. A strictly procedural conclusion. A perfect result, from a professional perspective. The ones who would ask questions of Edna Hamilton vanished into air.

But had they been permitted to ask, would truth have been the result? In cross-examination, it is the questions that matter more than the answers. To control the witness, to advance one's own theory of the case, that is the purpose of cross-examination that cannot be reconciled with the purpose of the question of my dream. Was there a single question that would have unlocked Edna's truth?

The last I ever heard from Edna Hamilton was her response to a letter I sent to her niece when I had gone looking for Edna Hamilton and learned she had moved:

I am at a loss to hear from my niece that you were looking for me. [As if my very curiosity were an impertinence.] I moved to Regina, having heard that my apartment was going to be taken down and there being no reason to stay in Toronto anyway.

I would very much appreciate it if the balance of funds in trust were sent to me direct, since I have no need to go to Toronto at the present time. Thanking you for your kindness to me and trusting to hear from you soon about the money.

Yours truly,

Edna Hamilton

At eighty-five years of age, alone and single, Edna had packed up and left.

The hand that wrote to me was rounded and firm. The proportions and shape of the letters appeared to my eye what the handwriting expert had said of exhibits "A" and "B" when examined against the sample handwriting given at Edna's discovery: "significantly similar…consistent with the conclusion that the sample was written by the same person years earlier."

But who was that person? Who do my questions of her reveal but her questioner—possibilities of self only I have been able to conceive?

the superintendent

"THIS BUILDING," HE says, "You can hear a pin drop." Grinning at her, he runs a thick tongue along his lip.

From the moment he invited her into the dark basement flat, she has been wary. At the superintendent's kitchen table, she stares at his window. It is placed high, near the ceiling. Grass grows at the sill. She wonders how anyone can live like this, with grass growing at eye level. It is as if he is already half-buried, living underground with the roots. He even looks like a mole—all whiskery and grey, with small furtive eyes. The only reason Franny tolerates this man is because he has an apartment for rent. She needs an apartment for the friend coming east in a month. From the street, the building had looked like something her friend could afford.

On the way home from work, Franny left her business card in the superintendent's mailbox, her home phone number on the back. She knows from past apartment hunts that vacancy rates depend upon what one does for a living. He may be coming here for her, but when he gets here, he'll be unemployed. If her friend gets an apartment in her city, it will be because *she* is a *lawyer*.

The phone was already ringing as she came through the door. The superintendent told her he might have a bachelor.

Nothing definite. He'd have to see her in person. His voice sounded secretive and boozy.

She had met her Vancouver lover when she was twenty-five. She had spent that summer in his city, where his love for her had been an unexpected gift. But when summer was over, she returned to her own city in the East. She does not know now why she returned. It was not to enter law school (she would not do that for another two years). But law school became one reason to stay.

"Let's take involvement first," he wrote to her in a letter when they were trying to decide what to make of their unlikely affair. "There must be some reality to our relation-ship. You are about to become a lawyer, and I am headed into the bush to teach Canada's indigenous peoples on this coast—what involvement can there be? We've talked about the geography between us before. If you find my language hard to take, I hope you also realize my effort at integrity in this letter. Let's not become separated by unrealistic expectations. We can trust a friendship that has lasted, now, years."

She did trust it, enough to let him come to her that Christmas. She trusted it over the next five years, enough to meet him in the hotel lobbies of strange cities. He loved her in a way that was always familiar and new, until she thought she could go on like this forever.

And then, unexpectedly, he announced his move: "If, for any reason, you decide our relationship is impossible, after I have moved to your city, there will be no reason for troubling your conscience. You are not responsible. This may seem like a simplistic notion, but it makes me more comfortable doing the thing I am going to do anyway, no matter what you say."

She puts the carton of milk she purchased on the way over on the superintendent's kitchen table—a signal: milk needs refrigeration. But the superintendent is taking his time, sucking every now and then on his bottle of beer.

"The apartment is not for me," she announces. "It's for a friend."

The face changes, taking on a narrow, suspicious look.

"A friend?"

"He's coming from the West Coast in a month. He's very responsible."

"I thought it was for you," he says accusingly.

"No, I told you that on the phone."

She did not tell him that on the phone, but the superintendent is less than sober. If he can forget what he just told her, she reasons, can he not also forget what she has *not* told him?

"No," he says emphatically. "You did not tell me on the phone."

"Well," she says finally, tiring of the game, "you know now."

"I thought it was for you," he sulks.

"Well, it is, in a sense. I'll be guaranteeing the lease." This, she realizes with horror, is precisely what she does not want to do.

"Now if it were for you," he says, "I wouldn't hesitate." Then he tells her he has two legal secretaries in the building. He has a "big case" coming up—motor vehicle. "A big case," but will not say any more. He sits back and blinks primly, lips buttoned, filled with a sense of his own importance. Is she supposed to be interested?

"It's not my specialty," she tells him flatly.

"Oh," he says, "what kind of lawyer are you?"

"Matrimonial."

"This is a very quiet building," he says, back to promotion. Then his voice drops and becomes conspiratorial. "What you two do when the door is closed is your own business."

At that, she stands up.

"Don't you want to see the place?"

"Well, yes. Are you going to show it to me?"

He stands up too. The heavy cluster of keys hanging from his belt threatens to pull down his pants.

"Just a minute," he says, "I'll tell the wife we're leaving."

She had no idea there was a wife hidden in the back room. He calls out to her as they leave the flat, telling her he's locking the door, not to answer if anyone knocks. No voice comes back in reply.

Together they wander the hallways, which are long and airless. But the carpet appears to have been recently vacuumed. That much is good. Whatever his finances, she does not want him to live in a hole.

The first time they made love, it was on his bare floor. They had come back to his apartment after an evening swim. She wore a cotton dress. Her damp hair blew in the wind behind her, and she swung her satchel saucily, with its weight of wet towel and bathing suit. He read her accurately, the message in that cotton dress wrapping about her unencumbered limbs. He claimed her the moment they got inside his door. All the windows in his apartment were open. Someone in the neighbourhood was cutting grass, and the air that blew over them smelled like sweet watermelon. Now every apartment she has scrutinized since has been measured for its capacity to accommodate such a scene.

The superintendent pauses at this door, now that door, tilts his head and listens intently. At one door, she hears the faint sound of a radio, at another, voices and a television set. She thinks of the people living behind these doors, all unsuspecting of the two of them listening at their lives. Whether in horror or fascination, she allows herself to be drawn along.

Outside one door, the superintendent stands back and rocks unsteadily on his heels. He spreads his legs for support, like an artist before his canvas, stands back and cocks a hip. With one hand on the hip, the other waving at the door, he tells her, "Miss Hartley here," as if Miss Hartley is indeed there and present in the flesh, "has been living here seventeen years. A Christian lady, Miss Hartley is, very Christian."

At another door: "One-o-six," he says, pinching the bridge of his nose in an effort to remember, "One-o-six. Oh, yeah, them's the ones I'm evicting."

He leads her to the elevator. "No one lives in this building but comes through me." He stares at her fixedly while they wait for their floor. "I've got to like 'em first," he says. A dubious honour, she thinks.

"I'm taking you to meet the first superintendent of the building. Miss O'Driscoll. She's ninety-six."

There are two other tenants visiting this ancient lady at the time. The one who answers the door is herself at least seventy.

Franny is embarrassed to find herself led into the living room, thick with the smell of boiled cabbage. As if he owns the place, the superintendent tells her to look around. She apologizes to the women. She does not have to look around, she says, can see that it is very spacious and well lit.

With their eyes all upon her, she finds her gaze drawn to a portrait above the couch. Richly framed, it suggests a former wealth nowhere else in evidence in the room. It is the photograph of a young man and woman at the turn of the century. The woman is of an astonishing beauty. Her eyes gaze at some point just above the camera's lens, which gives her the look of an immigrant before landing, or of a visionary. The man looks not at the camera, but at her. She is all his destination. It is a powerfully intimate moment.

"What a beautiful woman," Franny says aloud.

"Yes, isn't she," says the withered stranger on the couch. "That was my mother. It was taken before they came from Ireland."

What became of her? She is burning to ask, but knows this impoverished room is part of the answer.

When her lover first suggested this move to her city, Franny made a decision to stop writing. The comment in his letter that crystallized her decision was about food: "I've been too extravagant," he wrote, "in some of my indulgences—especially food. Today while I was at the market I couldn't resist the impulse to buy a stuffed boneless quail with some kind of glaze on it—an indulgence I can ill afford." She wrote back a six-page letter. What the panicked prose was all about could be summarized in a line: "I don't want to be poor."

In her years of struggle, she had learned her lesson well. What it was like to do without; what it was like to resist the "indulgence" of certain foods. Her determination to become a lawyer had, in part, been fuelled by this fear, and by the resolve not to depend on any man for her own survival.

She realized that poverty was a possibility he faced in his move to her city, a move he made for her sake, whatever he might say about responsibility. She feared he would fail. She could not bear the thought of his failure, of her disappointment, the guilt she would feel in being disappointed at all. And yet, so terrified was she of that possibility, she decided to foreclose on it altogether: "I wish I could believe you would prove me wrong. You once asked me what level of success you had to achieve before I would live with you, before I could feel safe? You also said there must be some reality to our relationship. I think reality is something we create. I don't know that you and I want the same reality."

A few months later, he announced the move. He did not ask for her help.

"I'm going to divorce my wife," the superintendent is saying to the women beneath the portrait, "so I can marry you, Miss Blake, or you, Miss Matthews." They titter like schoolgirls at his drunken attempt at charm, but behind the toothless grins, she notices something else—a strange fear. What possible power could this repulsive little man have over them to make them put up with his intrusions and pretend to enjoy his stupid jokes? Perhaps they are afraid that if for any reason he ceases to *like* them, to be amused, he will have them put out. Is it possible he has that kind of power over their lives?

"Am I going to see this apartment now?" Franny asks when they are once again out in the hallway.

Knocking very loudly, he hollers "Superintendent" like a policeman before breaking down a door. The woman who lives behind this door must have been tweezing hairs off her chin or squeezing pimples when they interrupted, for she holds a Kleenex up to her face. She is wearing a blue nylon housecoat that matches the light of the television flickering at her back.

"So you're making a move?" she asks the housecoated occupant conversationally.

"Oh, no," both the super and the occupant answer at once.

"This is an *example* of a bachelor," he adds.

She apologizes to the woman for the interruption. At the limit of her patience, she tells the superintendent she has seen enough, has got to be going, she has an appointment to keep.

He sees her to the door, and then on to the front lawn, still keeping her with his talk. He is telling her now about the time the absentee landlord sent over a friend whom he, the superintendent, turned away. "You don't have to live here, Mr. Silver," says I. "Nobody lives in this building but comes through me. I've got to like 'em first. When your friend comes from the West, you bring him to me."

It's all she can do to keep from running.

When she arrives back at her own apartment, she nearly weeps from relief. She stands at the door and surveys her place. There is the couch with its blue and violet pattern, the mahogany library table, the wing-backed chair, the Persian carpet, the many books. Everything in its place. An order to everything. The one she has imposed. Why, then, does she feel so unutterably depressed?

Whatever the cause, its effects are something she must rid herself of immediately. She opens the hall clothes cupboard. On his last trip to her city, her lover left a suit and two shirts in this cupboard. Opening it the morning after he left, she had recognized his smell—potent and male—even glanced back over her shoulder, half expecting him to be there. She knew his omission to pack these things was deliberate. He was moving closer by degrees.

She eventually took the shirts to be cleaned. But the night after his departure, she did something irrational. She slept in his shirt. She curled up inside it and hugged herself and tucked her nose into the underarm where his scent was the strongest, and cried herself to sleep.

He did not ask for her help. Knowing him as she did, she even knew he did not want her to hunt for this apartment. He would do that for himself. *The thing I am going to do anyway, no matter what you say.* The thing over which she had so little control. She realized that what she did this evening she did *for herself.* The realization, like the gift of his love for her, caught her by surprise.

She takes his shirt from the cellophane. Alone in the hallway of her apartment, she undresses. Then she dresses again in his shirt. It is the first sensible thing she has done all evening.

getting off lightly

SHE IS HEADED toward a corner. She sits in the passenger seat beside her recent husband, Zachary. She is pregnant for the second time. Her first miscarried. She and Zack weren't married at the time of the pregnancy or miscarriage. She had agreed to marry Zack only when she learned she was pregnant. But a few weeks before the scheduled wedding, the miscarriage occurred. In the hospital, Zachary had placed his bald head in her lap and wept into her hospital gown. He said of the lost baby, "At least our dear little one got us together. We made a commitment to each other. We bought a house." She heard his unspoken fear — that now the child was lost, she would be too. Moved to pity by the tears of the man weeping into her lap, she responded to his pain: "Don't despair, I will have your baby one day."

They are driving now toward the corner of Hastings and Main in Vancouver, where another man waits for her under a clock.

In the letter she wrote to this other man four months ago, she said: "I will be travelling to Vancouver with my husband, and I have already discussed with him the fact that I would

[86]

like to see you again. I will understand if, for whatever reason, *you* do not wish to see *me*."

That morning, she had asked Zack to let her off a block early, not wanting to meet the other man again under Zack's eyes. Zack promised. But he drives now right up to the corner. As she gets out of the car, she looks not toward the man she is going to meet, but back at the car. She sees her husband scanning the sidewalk for the man who might fit her descriptions. She refuses herself to look for the man, to lead Zack to him with her eyes. Instead, she stands on the corner, her arms crossed, cheeks flushed with anger, willing Zack to drive away. Only when the car pulls out from the curb and back into traffic do her eyes find him.

He leans against the wall, with a line-up of men leaning against the wall, making no move to come forward, to single himself out. She knew she could count on him. He is looking past her to the car. She supposes he is thinking: So that's the man you chose. "Did he come to you, prick forward, or use an approach more indirect?" This man who had told her years ago, "Be careful for yourself. Men will consider you a catch, a woman who can take care of herself, who carries herself through life like a snail with its own shell upon its back." Had she not known he too was a snail, she might have thought he warned her against himself.

This man, she had loved. Who would not marry her. Not anyone. What need of a wife, when he could do everything for himself? He said that before she knew he had had a wife, once, and a child, had himself raised the child with the help of a maiden sister who took the boy between sea voyages. Part of her believed he only said that about not needing a wife to protect himself against need. She was one year into her law practice when he came east to visit her. They were driving through downtown Toronto when she said: "I want a house like that." He stopped the car and backed up, surprising her with his interest in any house. It was an old townhouse, with a caged tree surrounded by interlocking brick. She liked the narrow, courtyard feel amid the density of city living. Shyly, she had asked him, "Would you live with me there, if I bought a house like that?" His only answer was a sort of snorting laugh. How ridiculous the question had been. She saw him standing solitary on the deck of his ship, his grey eyes staring out toward a night sea—feeling wind, feeling solitude—his own balance set against nothing. He would never live with her in her city house, the one she did eventually buy with her own money.

"Your letter said you had cut it." His eyes circle her hair, never meeting her eyes. "I'm glad to see it's still long."

He does not look at her directly. In all their times together, he has rarely looked at her directly. He has this way of seeing a thing whole, by casting his eyes about it, like a net. He hasn't noticed yet she is pregnant.

She got pregnant on her birthday. Zack woke her up singing with that boyish playfulness of his she thought would one day make him such a good father: "Happy birthday to you, you live in a zoo, with the elephants and the monkeys,

[88]

and I love you." She had thought: he wants a child. Although he had not said a word about it since the miscarriage, she knew it always. If truth were told, the miscarriage had been a relief to her. She was afraid to have a child. Zack knew that too. He had told her if it came to a choice between never having children and having her, he would choose her. That morning of her thirty-seventh birthday, hearing Zack sing, she had suddenly reversed herself.

She looks up at the clock. "Zack is picking me up back here in a couple of hours. We're taking the 2:30 ferry to Victoria. We have a couple of hours."

"I'll take you down to the quay. We'll walk some shore-line."

At four months, she doesn't really show yet. She is wearing her blue-jean dress — the one that hugs her torso and hips and then furls out in a long, full skirt. She wears it with a low-slung, country-and-western-style belt, studded with fake gems. City casual. City slick.

They walk in silence. And then he says, "You haven't gained any weight." He says it approvingly. She wondered if he would know. Years ago, when he had to reassure her she was not pregnant, he had told her: "You don't *look* like a pregnant woman." "What does a pregnant woman look like?" she had asked him. "Like a sleeping fish," was his answer. It is on the tip of her tongue to ask now: "Don't I look like a sleeping fish?" when he says:

"You look grand."

She is suddenly so grateful to him, she wants to weep. What is it about this man that always melts her heart? Is it because he loved her at a time when she was so unlovable — for no reason at all — like sending her the dozen roses the day before she married Zack? Love always, he had said in the note. Simple. Inexplicable. Love always. Yet she had no doubt it was true.

She keeps silent. This is not the way she wants to tell him.

They come to some train tracks. They are out of the seedy part of town and into an area where there seems to be no one, just storage shacks, landfill, and weeds. It is ugly, desolate. Where is he taking her? Why has he brought her here?

She is suddenly gripped with fear. Not for herself. For that other one — the life inside her. The same fear she used to feel so often when they first met. Fear of him, of his silence. *Who are you? Where are you from? Where are you going? I am myself, alone. I am what you see.* And what did she see? With that clouded fish vision of hers? Seeing always from the sides of her head. She had seen all sorts of things — a criminal, perhaps a murderer, someone running from a past, someone who would not unlock the storehouse of his memory, nor reveal himself, no matter how hard she tried. No amount of cross-examination would avail. She had feared him. And yet with this fear, she had given herself to him, over and over again. Because she had wanted to die. At least part of her wanted to die. That summer in Vancouver. The other part left notes in her wallet, on her telephone message pad — places the police might look if she went missing. She would rip up the notes on returning home safely, only to remake them again the next time when he called her days or weeks later. Where had he been? No answer. They could talk about their past together, the past they were creating. The past they created over the next ten years. And what they wrote to each other, the scenes they painted in each other's minds, became as real as the moments together, for those engraved images upon their imaginations that grew over time. So he had been with her on holiday to Avignon, brushing her long hair at an open window, shooing a pigeon away with the back of her brush, and she had been with him on board his commercial trawler, playing chess with some mate, watching islands approach like ghosts from the mist.

And when he came east to her city, the first time she would let him visit her in her city, she had trembled as if from some bitter cold as she told him how very close she had come *to that*. She had lowered her voice and gritted her teeth, lest someone in the restaurant hear her blasphemy — how there had been a time when she had hated her life. That was the one time he had looked at her directly, taking her hand, gripping her with his eyes: "You must never do that. That is not the way you will leave me." Then he had counselled: "To stay sane, study birds, study fish, study anything." So she had decided to study law.

"Did he walk toward you, prong forward, as in a game of blind man's bluff? Or did you again orchestrate the affair, making sure *that he too fell in love with you*?"

If the truth were told, she had been dying from loneliness, for the want of someone to love.

But apart from their beginning, when for the space of one summer she had lived in his city, they saw each other rarely. She would not return to the West. He could not move inland, away from his port city. In the meantime, he raised his son; she went to law school. She began a career that committed her to staying put.

"I am honestly pleased to know you are happy, as you could not have been with me: crazier than a March rabbit, and woollier than a coyote, prick avowedly polygamous. I saw that I could never offer you what you desired...."

He has gone ahead of her, down a small incline beside the train track. Feeling her not beside him, he turns around, assesses her hesitation, and then holds out his hand. She takes it. It is the first time this day they have touched—a non-touch—not like the solid grip of their past. He guides her over the rocks and landfill, down toward the shore, the two of them looking not at each other, but down at her shoes—the delicate, white laceups with their thin soles she had polished this very morning, while Zack watched her grimly over his coffee and promised to let her off a block early.

"There is always the risk, with this type of thing, that you might meet someone else," he had said to her on one of his last visits to her city. He had said "you," not "you or I," as if there was no issue it would never be him.

"What would you do?" she had asked him.

"I would be heartbroken," he had said.

"Would you fight for me?"

"I would not fight for you."

That he would not fight for what he wanted, that he could give her up so easily, made her angry.

"I don't suppose there's any point in asking if you would still see me this way?"

"No," she had answered without hesitation. "I would never do that."

"I didn't think so."

"I'm not that sort of woman. I know who I am. I would never do that to any husband I married."

"I didn't think so."

They made love that night, as if for the last time. Every time they made love, it was as if for the last time. It was spring, and she had left the windows open. It had rained all day and the air was fresh with the smell of worms, the sound of cars passing on a wet city street. They made love and part of her died with him again, as it did every time. Afterward, she lay under him like a crushed animal. He leaned over her and stroked her face, very gently, with the back of his hand.

"What?" she asked, looking up at him, at his eyes glistening down at her in the dark.

"It kills me to think of you making love like that to any other man."

"I never will."

"Never say never," he had said. "We never know what we might do."

"I *know*," she had answered the man with confidence, "I know who I am."

So he knew, when she wrote to him about Zack, that it was over for them.

"Something has happened," she wrote, "Although we have not corresponded in over a year, I feel I owe you the knowledge."

She told him about Zack, typing up her description of him as if she were setting out his qualifications for a job. "Zack is a real estate and corporate lawyer," she began. "He is also an avid gardener. He has just gone outside in the autumn rain, pushing a wheelbarrow with a rhododendron for transplanting to the front of our house. (We had the front garden terraced this fall, with a lot of stonework.) My husband is a gardener. He has grown his winter beard. I admit to loving him more with his beard than without it. I am sitting at my kitchen table as I write this, looking out at the backyard through the solarium, where I have my plate rack. It is there he will start his seed trays in the winter for the spring plant. I feel such gratitude to him, watching him go by with the wheelbarrow, intent upon his gardening, totally unaware of the betrayal in his wife's quick little fingers."

In the same letter, she told him about having cut off her long hair. She told him about her new house in an established neighbourhood, with its great maple tree in the back, how she loved that tree, had wrapped her arms half around it the day they moved in. "There is something else," she said in the same letter. "Although I thought I never wanted a child, the moment I learned I had conceived, I began to love the life growing in me. The loss of it was one of the hardest I have ever had to bear. Perhaps this is why I am telling it to you, to whom I have always been able to tell everything."

She and Zachary had married three weeks after the miscarriage. They married anyway. Who would have believed them—that they were marrying for love, with such haste, when seven months later she bore the child she now would never have? It seemed that with the loss of that child, she had fallen in love with Zack, who had not hesitated for a moment when she told him, who had blushed with pleasure and gone hard against her.

That was over three years ago, now. The cut roses arrived the morning before the wedding, with his simple note: "Love always." Just as forty roses would arrive years later for her fortieth birthday, and she would know, without a doubt, from whom they came.

He did not fight for her. And she had no doubt that she had broken his heart.

They are standing now on a dock, which juts past the ramshackle buildings out into the bay.

"On a weekday, this place is buzzing. I buy my fresh fish over there."

"We're renovating the house. We're doing over the basement, making it into a flat." She leaves out the word "nanny."

"Of course," he says simply, as if renovations were a fore-gone conclusion.

They look at each other and laugh. They laugh and laugh. His laughter reaches out and forgives her. It's all right, this laughter says, to want something so ordinary, to care about your floor tiles and the colour of your walls.

"You'll be fine," he says. "You look happy. Marriage obviously becomes you. You must have needed to be married."

She wants to hit him for that.

"Did you ever mean it when you told me you were going to move east?"

"Yes," he says simply.

"You never would have come."

"Wouldn't I?"

"We'll never know, will we?"

But he has said what she needed to hear, possibly what she came to hear. *I did not betray you, your conviction of who I was, what we were. It didn't come together as we hoped. It doesn't mean I didn't love you.*

"Having returned from a remote part of Pacific Rim National Park—a stay that started early July following my layoff—I realized I could no longer proceed according to the earlier plan." That was how he started his last letter to her. Was that supposed to explain it—the months of silence, after she had finally said "yes"—a process that had taken ten years? Ten years, while she had gone to law school, while his son had grown up, ten years to realize that the backs-and-forths were not enough, that she loved him, that she wanted to be married. "…I have rented a place and prepared for spending another winter here. It follows that my plans have been delayed, not changed. I do not presume that you will see it that way. I thought of returning the keys to your apartment in person. However, the prospect of arriving with bad news and who knows what kind of departure kept me from doing that. For that matter, I would rather that you came out west again for a change, if you will consider it anymore at this stage."

Coward, she had thought. Consider it? It was out of the question. She wrote back sharply:

"Your silence of almost two months prepared me for the disappointment contained in your last letter. It did not come as a surprise. What surprised me was that you could have deferred, until the last moment, telling me what you yourself must have known back in early July, when you say you were 'laid off.' I will not spend the fall as I spent this summer. I will not let you turn me bitter over what has been between us, nor give you the chance to make me regret ever having met you. I am ending this now."

And end it she did. Determined woman that she was. She went out and met Zack. That very November. It wasn't until Christmas that he let her have him. She did not "orchestrate their affair." Zachary knew her game. He was not going to let her out that lightly.

Zack. Who did not let her down. Who had flushed with pleasure and become hard when she asked him, "What does it feel like to hold a pregnant woman?" Words that sounded like the beginning of a riddle or a joke. Zack.

"What do you want from life?" she had asked him when she first met him. "That's easy," Zack said. "What everyone wants," he had answered.

"What is that?" she pressed. Was she finally going to have an answer?

"To be happy. To be rich."

He said this without irony, with the most uncomplicated grin.

"What do you want from life?" she had asked that other man, over ten years ago. He had said nothing, and then nothing. They were hiking together. They had come to a mountain lake and surprised two lovers laying naked on a rock. He said nothing. He looked across the lake as the lovers scrambled for their tent. He said nothing. And then nothing. She grew impatient. Finally, he had laughed—whether at the question or the sight of the lovers, she never knew which. Later that afternoon, he took her, standing with her back against a tree—his need so urgent, so pressing, it carved the tree into her back. Afterward he told her, "I used to want to be rich. I had this stupid dream to be a millionaire by thirty. That's before I learned the futility of all desire." She did not believe him. She openly disparaged his philosophy. "You're a coward," she accused. "Isn't it easier not to want, not to care—so much easier than to risk losing? How does one live without desire?" She did not believe him—that it was possible to make love like that without passion. And once to have had it, to be able to let go. *I will not fight for you.*

She had looked at Zack, with his simple grin. He wants to be happy. He wants to be rich. What would it be like to attach one's life to such a man, to want such simple things? To get through life in baby steps, one choice at a time—like what colour to paint one's kitchen walls?

Zack wanted a child. Zack wanted her.

She thought the two irreconcilable. "Marry someone younger," she had told him. Some women are mother material. I am not. Hadn't she known that about herself since the age of fifteen, watching a movie about childbirth in the medical pavilion at Expo '67, seeing the pulse of blood gush from between a woman's spread legs, the afterbirth? Never me, she had thought, *never me*.

Never say never. We never know what we might do.

The day the bleeding started, she had a court appearance out of town. All the way to Milton and back in a mounting snowstorm, she had thought: I am losing my baby, I am losing it because of this, because of people whose lives are not my life, who are nothing to me.

After court, she had gone to see a friend. Throughout the afternoon, she lay on the friend's couch, holding her cup of tea. She wanted so badly just to stay still, there in the friend's house, her hands around the cup, the cup in her lap. Her eyes closed and she fell asleep. She woke to find the friend had removed the cup and wrapped a blanket around her lap, did not seem to mind that she had fallen asleep in the midst of her story about the kids.

Never say never. You never know what you might do.

The next day, Zack came to pick her up at the hospital. "Why didn't you call me? You're such a strong woman," he said, "to go through that alone." She felt his unspoken fear — that now she would leave him, now there was no reason to stay. He knelt before her and put his head into her lap. While his sobs wet through her hospital gown, she stroked the bald dome of Zack's head. Zack wanted a baby. He wanted her. He knew so simply what he wanted. Wasn't it easier to give Zack what he wanted than to know it herself? At least to give Zack what he wanted was within reach.

The sun comes out — after weeks, apparently, of rain.

"You brought the sun with you."

They are walking back toward town in search of coffee.

"Let's sit outside. We get so little sun on the coast." He borrows a cloth from the waiter and wipes off two chairs and the table.

"Have you never felt alone — so alone you think you will die?"

Silence, as he considers.

"Motion helps. Wind in my face. I usually enjoy the journey."

She will tell him eventually. She will announce the birth of her son in a Christmas card — the son with whom she was pregnant that afternoon in Vancouver, that afternoon she went forward to look up her past.

"Sundays were the worst. Yet for all the loneliness I felt when I met Zack, I used to insist on those days alone, apart from him. And Zack always gave them to me. Without any resentment. The odd thing is, Zack also had this independence from me. For example, when I had my son, I didn't have to worry about Zack. He knew he had been completely eclipsed and just accepted it: as long as I was happy with my baby, it was fine by him that he was excluded from our orbit. I will always be grateful to him for that."

"I've taken to driving a motorcycle," the man wrote back: "Even in foul weather I do feel the urge, put on my Black Diamonds and steam my way through the Malahat mist, riding past midnight into the little hours. Summers I push it, seeing how much it can do, but the speedometer possibilities are, as usual, lies. On the flat, even downhill at full torque, it won't do much over one hundred miles. It does stand up on its back tire from a start, but I don't know how to do the trick very well, and the effort almost scares the shit out of me — and that, believe it or not, is cause for delight.

"The same bike has taken me 'off' the highway, although it is a street version. (It sat in my townhouse living room as the chrome conversation piece for the first winter.) But it went slip sliding on logging roads similar to which I was used to driving in earlier years, and it came out buzzing like a chocolate-coated insect. I drove it down long, dry washouts and ran it across a small river. The machine is five or six hundred pounds, so partway success on that obstacle was not possible. In fact I was surprised that it did not tilt midstream because it had kind of flipped around on some muddy trails elsewhere.

"On such occasions, feeling momentary euphoria because of so-called success with the bike riding, and because the experience is a wonderful mix of reality and fantasy, it is easy to ask: 'Is this *it*?' Equally easy for another, not involved, to quickly answer no, life is not about euphoria achieved in overcoming obstacles. Although I think of such things, the 'it' question does not organically come to me since I went to the beach. I think I mentioned to you at our last meeting that I spend weeks there, literally, and see no one. No footsteps over a mile and a half of sand for days. There, having often forgotten what day it is, or even forgotten to rate days in the abstract — that is, apart from foggy, rainy, windy, cold, warm or hot. There I have known that *it* is *it*, although I would not want to say it seriously, for fear of spoiling it.

"From the above you know that I have not worked for hire much. I taught again, hated it much worse than before, and quit. Still thinking about working in the food industry, but more likely I'll do my own. I've been developing a herring pickle. Like reinventing the wheel, you might say, but mine is better. The point I would make is my needs are little. For instance, sailing. Need or extravagance? Anyway, my neighbour on the little island, who is in the *Guinness Book of Records* for sailing around the world solo or some such thing and *who owes me*, will be coerced into taking me aboard the famous circumnavigating vessel he keeps at Thieves Bay. Furthermore, my sort of buddy, who works on the big island at a peeler bar as the tap man, *promised* me the use of his fishing vessel moored at the quay. My investment—rods, gear, mostly stuff I got for the Steelhead run in Stamp River earlier. Small needs. Might have to get a freezer, though, and a wheelbarrow to cart the salmon from the dockside to the house.

"Now for *more* of *what you did not ask about.* I fell in love once again, but it did not last. Never does, only the kids do. Speaking of kids, that is one sweet-looking boy in the photo. Hope you're not too busy to spend more than just 'quality time' with your son. Worst thing for people like you and me is to nanny them off. I guess that's because, among other things, we are people 'of the head,' meaning we have to, we just *have to know.* And what is there to know? Who we are going to live with (presumably) for the rest of our lives, what they are about...."

She is heading back toward a corner—"the corner of Hastings and Main, in Vancouver, where I will meet you. Under the clock...."

"Will you meet my husband? We could go to lunch together. He is a good man, Zack. I think you would like him."

"You're not going to make me go through that, are you?" he asks gently, without looking at her, looking over her, catching her whole in the net of his eyes.

"No," she says, "I won't ask." She knows that if she did, he would oblige her.

"But if you want a good restaurant..." and he tells her about this little hole-in-the-wall, which serves up succulent fried oysters.

She and Zack go there. But the oysters are a mistake.

They do catch the 2:30 ferry. On the way to Victoria, she is sick to her stomach. Motion does not help. When she emerges from the bathroom, limp from throwing up, there are tears in her eyes. Through her tears, she sees Zack out near the railing. He is looking out to sea. Unexpectedly, he turns and finds her, as if by instinct, like the needle of a compass finding north. The smile he gives her is one of pure delight. She is so grateful to him for this smile. Her recent husband. She rushes to join him. Pregnant again she is — this time by choice. Zack ropes an arm around her and kisses her eyes. Misinterpreting their moisture, he says gently, "You didn't think, now, you'd be getting off lightly?"

And for now, anyway, his kisses catch the tears.

unwanted gifts

FRANCESCA LIES ON a wooden lawn chair in the dead woman's garden. Tiffany's garden still, at least to Francesca, who will always think of it that way, although the tractor wheels have clawed through Tiffany's beds. The tulips Tiffany planted in seasons past are blooming yet miraculously in the grooves. With all this active construction, there is not a trace of Tiffany's death, of any violence, in Tiffany's garden.

Francesca and her husband are in Oakville this day to see how the renovations are progressing. This is something Tiffany had always wanted to do—renovate the house from top to bottom. How Tiffany hated the house—a suffocating, narrow house, with small, confining rooms. To see the house now, all opened up with windows and skylights, gold-plated fixtures in the bathrooms from their new Italian-importer friend, slate tiles in the kitchen where once dark wood had been.

Francesca lies on an old lawn chair in Tiffany's garden, thinking about her dead sister-in-law, about the tulips Tiffany planted, about the stones she placed around the bases of trees, looking at the excavations, thinking Tiffany must have rolled in her grave—if only she knew. If only she could see what was happening to the small house on the grand lot where she had borne her children, renovated now from top to bottom by her husband's new wife. And to imagine the new wife, Muriam, making such an investment in a dead woman's house. Poor Muriam. Poor Tiffany. It does not occur to Francesca yet to think "poor Francesca," although hasn't she, too, married a Hamilton?

"Hamiltons don't divorce their wives; they kill them." Was Francesca the only one to hear Muriam make that remark—drunk at her own engagement party—this dark allusion to her precursor's suicide?

The sun is wonderful in Tiffany's garden, the old wooden lawn chair warm and solid against Francesca's back. Francesca's small son plays now in the tree house, opening and closing imaginary doors. Francesca watches her son through half-closed eyes. Now he's down the ladder again and has found some marbles under an eavestrough opening. Francesca imagines Tiffany wondering what to do with the marbles her children had outgrown. She must have decided to put them there under the eavestrough, where a few years after her death, Francesca's first-born takes one and pockets it. An unintended gift.

Francesca remembers the bitterness in Tiffany's voice when her husband gave Francesca's husband a special bottle of wine for his birthday, just a few weeks before the wedding. "To your first-born," Tiffany had said, looking straight at Francesca. The way Tiffany said it, with that knowing little laugh, had made her words sound like a curse, like Tiffany couldn't wait for Francesca to have her first child: "*Then* you'll know," the eyes seemed to say. Know what? Francesca wondered. Later that night, she had told her future husband: "Their marriage is in trouble; she is deeply unhappy." "You think so?" he had said, incredulous. Francesca was the first to see it. But then, she saw it with an outsider's eyes. The separation. Not the death. Did anyone but Tiffany see that?

Francesca's first-born was a year old when Tiffany committed suicide.

Not a trace now of Tiffany in her own garden. Not a trace of any suffering, any violence, any death. Nothing. It is as if she has been eradicated. Francesca and her son are entirely safe, in the sunshine, in Tiffany's garden.

That morning Francesca had dug a deep hole in her own garden for the lilac she wanted planted. Francesca can hardly close her fingers for all the pruning and digging she has done this spring. That morning, the sight of a thick root sticking up out of the earth like a ventricle had made her sick. She wondered about the tender plant she was going to shove into that hole, if it would have a chance against all that old underground growth. This passion for gardening is something she has learned through her husband. The Hamiltons are all avid gardeners. Her mother-in-law's gardens had been legendary. Gardening must be in her own roots, too, for Francesca to take it up with such a passion. There will be no tomato sticks in her own garden. Rather, Francesca will have flowers, she tells her husband—a profusion of flowers all summer long, a real Victorian, perennial garden. She doesn't know the names of anything. She just wants lots of them, all summer long, year after year.

Tiffany never did see Francesca's first-born. Francesca and her husband drove up to the darkened house one Sunday evening in the early part of his brother's separation, just after the birth. It was an impulse of her husband, on the way back from a Hamilton Sunday dinner. "Do you think she'll *want* to see us? Francesca had asked. But her husband's self-centred joy was such at the time that he just assumed everyone must feel as he did at the birth of their son. To look at her son's innocent sleeping face, his peaceful little body strapped into the baby car seat, Francesca almost believed it was possible—that people could put their own pain aside to celebrate new life. Still, she had waited with her newborn in the car. A friend of Tiffany answered the door and told her husband that Tiffany wasn't "receiving visitors" that night.

"Fran, what are you thinking?" Francesca's husband calls from the frame of a sliding-glass doorway that will open out onto the new deck. "Fran," again, when the response is not instantaneous. She hates it when he interrupts her like this, the way he will snap his fingers into the face of their son, who might be lost in his world of blocks, then turn away just when he catches the boy's attention—the way he turns away now, with her brother-in-law, before she can answer, either not caring to know the answer or indifferent to the risks. Is that the reason she shouts after him: "I don't want a watch or a party for my birthday."

That is what her brother-in-law gave Tiffany for her fortieth birthday. A watch and a party — neither of which she wanted.

Even then, Francesca had been astonished at how wasted Tiffany appeared. It was the last time Francesca would ever see her. Tiffany and her husband separated not long after the party. Tiffany did it just months before her support cheques were scheduled to run out. Had she made it through the year, Tiffany would have been forty-three.

It was a "surprise" birthday party, her fortieth. Francesca's brother-in-law asked all of Tiffany's family and all of the Hamiltons. Francesca was a relatively "new" Hamilton at the time. The garden party was in this same garden. Tiffany sat on this very chair and was required to open her presents. During the present opening, Francesca leaned over and asked her husband what he had bought. Too busy that week to choose the gift, the responsibility for its purchase had fallen to her husband. He bought a mug. A single mug. "You can't be serious." Her husband smiled, so proud of himself at this mean-spirited, vindictive little gift.

Four mugs were what Tiffany had bought for their wedding. Francesca married into the Hamiltons at Thanksgiving and that first Christmas received combined wedding and Christmas gifts. As it was her first Hamilton Christmas,

Francesca had been required to open their presents, to sit on a chair surrounded by Hamiltons, just as Tiffany did on her fortieth birthday. The worst of it was that it was all so very public, all the Hamiltons watching to see how she would react. Francesca did not know how to react. She had hated the mugs. But more than the mugs themselves, she could not believe the meanness of the gift—that it should be a wedding and Christmas gift, combined.

By Tiffany's fortieth birthday, only one of the four mugs remained. It survived as a container for holding Francesca's paints. But never, never would Francesca have thought to reciprocate in kind. Each Christmas, Francesca continued to gift the Hamiltons, undaunted by the penuriousness and practical ugliness of the gifts that came back. It was a question of *who she was*. She could not give such a gift. Had her husband no shame? Francesca fled into the house, just as Tiffany reached for their gift.

Her husband later said that Tiffany did not react at all. She could not have remembered, he said. Not for a moment did Francesca believe that. She remembered, all right.

How could they ever have thought Tiffany would "receive" them?

Sitting in Tiffany's garden, in her chair, the chair from which Tiffany had been made to open all their gifts, Francesca wonders about Tiffany's wedding gift to them—what could have prompted the mugs? Francesca's father-in-law had called Tiffany "one of the most honest women I have ever known."

If Tiffany were honest, then the mugs had to be honest too, a true expression of the "honest" Tiffany at the time. What did they say?

Whatever it was, it was a message everyone had missed.

There's a clatter of bicycles in the driveway as Graham arrives home with a friend. They dump the bikes, not even bothering with the kickstands. The back wheels spin like the last spasms of a dying animal. Francesca's first-born turns toward his cousin Graham, older than him by seven years. He runs with hands cupped and outstretched before him, as if carrying something of incredible delicacy.

"Graham, look. Do you see it?"

"What?"

"The Mommy spirit?"

"The what?"

"Remember in *Land Before Time,* the water in the leaf? The air in my hands is the Mommy spirit."

Francesca's first-born holds his cupped little hands up to his cousin, inviting him to look. Graham looks down at his cousin with an expression impossible to read. The friend twitches with restlessness at his side.

"Sure, kid," Graham says, and gives Francesca's first-born a pat before heading off with the friend into the house. He never does take a look.

There had been a family gathering at Tiffany's cottage the summer after her death. Francesca shared the early mornings with her son and Graham alone. Graham was about seven at the time—the only Hamilton to rise early in the morning. They spoke in whispers, so as not to disturb the other Hamiltons. Sometimes they would not speak at all. In fact, Graham had an amazing capacity for silence in one so young—he would make his way down to the kitchen as quiet as a mouse, surprising Francesca with his presence. The first morning, Francesca had watched him go to the cupboard for cereal and a bowl, and thought of what her mother-in-law had told her about finding Tiffany in bed while "Poor little Graham ate cereal downstairs from the box, no one even to pour his milk."

"Would you like me to make eggs for you?" Francesca offered. Graham looked up at her, surprised. Perhaps it was his lack of expectation, or the gratefulness with which he had devoured her eggs, that first endeared Graham to Francesca. Graham, with his silence.

"Graham," Muriam had called to him from the deck of the cottage, persistently, over and over again. Muriam had just returned from town, with a book on insects she wanted to give him. Graham and Francesca were hidden from view by the overhang of bush. "Graham," the voice rang out, becoming more urgent now, touched with impatience. Graham looked at Francesca. They both knew the other had heard. Neither gave the other away.

At least in Graham, Tiffany had one who would remember, in whom she would not be so easily replaced.

Years later, Francesca would hear herself make a joke of it: "I asked only one thing of my husband that summer. I wanted a garden. Give me a garden, I said to my husband. It wasn't until summer was over that I realized why my grass was never cut. He was gardening, all right, but not *my* garden. Her name was Brenda." Francesca would watch the faces of her listeners, the sudden realization. Then reserve, as they waited for Francesca's own reaction. Then Francesca would laugh, and her listeners along with her. A distanced laugh. For by then, Francesca would have survived it all: The pain, the betrayal, the return of herself. Like an envelope marked: "Return to sender. Address unknown."

Francesca's husband will not give Francesca a party for her fortieth birthday. Nor will he give her a watch. Years later, Francesca will try to remember what he did give her for that birthday, but will only be able to remember the grief. She does, however, remember what he gave her for their tenth wedding anniversary, in the year she turned forty-three.

It will come into the house months earlier, in a different form, dredged up from the Hamilton basement and smelling of it, given to them when her in-laws decided to move house — their unwanted chess table.

The chessboard itself will be made of marble, a beautiful salmon and cream-coloured marble, with onyx pieces. But the marble board will be mounted in an ugly yellow frame, with conical legs and industrial-looking casters. The wood itself looks pressed, not even real, and one of the legs will be missing. It will have to be reconceived.

But oh, what Francesca sees! Alexander's game, a game played in flapping tents — impermanent encampments on the

eve of battle—a strategist's game, which, like the encampments themselves, must be continuously taken up, realigned
depending on the play. She will see something in dark
mahogany, but light, which can be folded at a moment's
notice, the pieces collapsed into cases that will hang at the
table's side, a small portable thing, like one's own life.
Francesca will phone her poet friend, who is also a carpenter.
Together, they design. But before the work can be finished,
the anniversary will arrive—her tenth anniversary in her
forty-third year—and with it, the gift.

It will sit in the middle of her living room, doubling for a
coffee table—a solid, immovable slab of wood the length of a
small door, the marble board sunk into its face. The pieces
will lie in shallow graves against green felt. Tears on a birthday or anniversary bring bad luck. But Francesca will not be
able to keep back the tears. Her young son will hang from
her knees and will try to pluck her hands down from her
face. "Momma, what's the matter? Don't cry," and still
Francesca will not be able to stop crying.

This day, in Tiffany's garden, those tears are far away—
three years, at least. There is no trace of tears yet in Tiffany's
garden. Nor of Tiffany, who gave back her life this past
spring. What moves Francesca in Tiffany's garden is not
Tiffany's ghost, nor even the knowledge that she must move,
cannot stay forever still, with her back planted against this
chair. It is the chill that rises through the emptiness between
the slats. The earth exhales as the afternoon shortens. Its chill
enters her from behind.

Francesca rises suddenly, and calls to her son.

vivi's florentine scarf

VIVI PUT ME up to buying the scarf at a marketplace in Florence. She was a much older woman than I, nearly twice my age, and my hesitation angered her. In view of the price (even on my student's budget, this was a bargain), Vivi could not fathom what was keeping me from possession. The scarf was bright, almost gaudily coloured, and large—more of a sarong than a scarf. "But what will I use it for?" "Use? Why anything—to wrap yourself when you step out of the bath, *for your man.*" There was no man in my life at the time. Single, I towelled down after a bath. This scarf would not blot a drop. I had learned from the other students that Vivi was married to a rich German engineer, had four adult sons. She travelled alone that summer, as did we all, purportedly studying *Quattrocento* art in Italy. The notion of the scarf, the bath, and the man was totally impractical. Still, the vision stayed with me because Vivi could see it, where I could see only her impatience with me, not what prompted it—my own youthful preparedness to waste.

Vivi, dying of cancer, although undiagnosed at the time, took the scarf from the market vendor and threw it about herself passionately. The Florentine sun caught the gold threads between colours and the scarf transformed her.

"If you don't, I will."

Professor Lucke's first lecture (the only one to be in a class-room; all the rest will be in churches, monasteries, graveyard chapels, before the objects of our collective gaze): "Why Tuscany? Why murals? Italy is the cradle of Western civiliza-tion and Tuscany participates in this fruitful exercise. It is the nature of mural painting that promises to remain faithful to the original location of the image by the nature of the word 'mural'—wall. Wall painting needs a technique. Fresco—'fresh'—a technique in which paint is applied to wet plaster. The pigment undergoes, because of wetness, a process of intense binding. The result is a painting of remarkable solidi-ty, with the capacity to face the attacks of time. The mural, like love, is not transferable. It keeps us, holds us, wants our response. This art, it speaks to me. I cannot hear it. I just see the lips move. It is as if, through the ages, the sound gets lost. I try to find the bridge from here to there. I don't understand because the language has been lost, like faith itself."

Professor Lucke tries to find a way back, to find it for him-self. For every time he speaks to us, it is as if he is in intimate dialogue with himself.

Why Tuscany? Why murals? Does this answer for any one of us, his followers, why we were here? Why am I in Italy that summer—the summer before I start my legal career? *I do not know what this thing is, my life. I do not know what purpose it has, what to make of it.* To stay sane, study birds, study rocks, study anything. So I travel about Italy, with those firm, slender limbs, studying the "Allegory of Obedience," Giotto, Andrea del Sarto, Fra Bartolommeo, the upper and lower churches of Assisi, with the same lost intensity as I have studied law.

"Painting catches a moment. Prose flows like time. At a certain moment, Christ says, 'There is a Judas among us. There is one who will betray me.' Is this the moment the artist will choose, or the one when Christ first breaks bread, transforming it with meaning? What moment do you choose?"

It must have been obvious for Eva to say to me after class, "The thirties are the most awful time for a single woman."

She had watched me talk to Branko after class — Branko, who in Rome had told me about his anonymous encounters with men under bridges at night, one turned to horror at knife-point. "Life offers us nothing but a series of opportunities to feel ashamed." Branko would not put his arm around me at the Baths of Caracala when an open-air performance of Tosca turned cold. Shamelessly, I had asked him to hold me. On the bus back to Rome, I had told him how, at thirty-two, I still sometimes went home to my parents for a hug. He said, "You know, sometimes you make me feel very sad. I could give you a hug, but it wouldn't be honest."

As we walked down the stairs from class together, Branko told me about the man he had just met. They had gone out last night and had dinner together, for hours. Now the man was helping him find an apartment in Siena. Generous in his happiness, Branko lavished me with a consoling little hug. I wanted to smack him.

Eva must have diagnosed my malady, for on the way back

to residence, she said what she said about a woman in her thirties.

"In her thirties, a woman goes through an almost unbearable physical suffering if she has no mate. It is the first time you realize you may never find one and may never have a child. By forty, you have usually reconciled yourself to that thought. You don't suffer over it as much."

Eva had retired from nursing that year. She and I shared a bathroom at the *conservatori feminili* in Siena. There was a man Eva had loved in her late thirties, and who had wanted to marry her, but Eva had not made that choice for herself. He was ten years her junior. Whatever the reason, Eva made a decision against the man.

"Did you ever regret it?"

"No. It was not the man I regretted. I met him years later, and knew I had not made a mistake. *It was the child.*" She said this matter-of-factly, as was her way, so that I almost missed it.

"You had a child?"

"No. *The child I never had.*"

Professor Lucke, who professed himself to be without belief yet daily stood a starved man before a banquet table where he could not eat, compares two paintings of the same subject—a Guido da Siena and Duccio Madonna with child. In the first, both mother and child are preciously dressed, faces composed of geometrical forms. The child is less of a child than the visualization of an idea, our Saviour, who is Saviour the moment he is born. In the Duccio, the child is a baby. Again the mother holds the child in her left arm, but the baby has grasped a little bit of her cloak. Such a human gesture! You see the childlike playfulness of the gesture of her right hand, the way the mother holds these little feet. She holds a child's feet in her hands, at the same moment as she holds the feet of the crucified Christ. "Look at us and behold; we are human, he is human. You can come to me because I am a mother. This is my little child. I know about you because *I have gone through that.*"

The night before this lecture, I have a dream I am in labour, the birth pains pulling me to earth like the force of gravity. It is not the pain of a menstrual period. It is rather as if some-one has reached up inside me, taken hold of my womb, and is tearing me out—a cutting, annihilating pain. I wake on the single bed in my cell-like room, knowing my pregnant sister back in Canada must be in labour. I wake, relieved that it is she and not I, for I am terrified of her pain. I do not want this cup for myself, nor do I want to pass through life alone. In the terror of this night, these seem two irreconcilable fears.

Coming back to residence with Eva, I find the telegram and know, without opening it, that my sister's child has come.

"Look and behold, we were human. He was human. You can come to me, because I am a mother and this is my little child. I know about you, because I have gone through that."

And I thought what he meant was the pain of childbirth,

never for a moment conceiving far worse. No, because in *this* painting, at *this* moment, the mother holds the child's feet in her hands. *"Ah," said my son's eventual father, watching me play with the little feet of my only son. "You kiss those feet now. Don't you know those are the feet that will take him away from you?"*

She holds the child's feet in her hands, at the same moment as she holds the feet of the crucified Christ.

Vivi is difficult to describe. Even her age is indeterminate. She might be sixty-five or fifty. She has been a model, has sold real estate, even taught—this in addition to having mothered four sons. Her pregnancies were terrible, with an overactive thyroid not diagnosed until she was in her late forties. She is Estonian—a tall, skinny blond woman, who does her makeup well, who dresses elegantly in melon-coloured silk dresses she made on her own—always elegant and womanly, with an innate artistry.

We met returning to the *Conservatori Feminili Reuniti* late one afternoon. Recognizing each other from class, we went to Nannini's for tea. She seemed lonely, though in my ignorance I could not imagine how someone could be lonely in a life of such density. She said she had a decision to make about that night. Her taxi driver had asked her for a date. She was nervous about agreeing because her Italian was insufficient to lay the ground rules for the evening; on the other hand, she wanted to break out of the circle of females at our residence. I told her I wished for male company, too. I told her about Branko, and how it was frustrating to be frequently with a male who elicited female response, but had no male response.

She said she really wished she could meet someone gay, that she loved gay men — they were so intuitive.

The next day in Florence, Vivi saw me with Branko and ran after us. She announced that she wanted to have a really good meal with people who looked as if they weren't afraid to spend some money. At lunch, we had wine, perhaps were all a little drunk. Vivi talked and talked. At one point, she pretended to a weakness she did not have, and placed her hand on Branko's arm, as if for support. Branko preened at her touch.

"I do not believe you. You are a very strong woman," I said.

"You know that? I do not like the idea of being known."

On the bus, that evening, we sat separately — Branko way in the back, Vivi behind me. At one point, I turned around to hear something Vivi was trying to tell me, and Branko caught my eye, behind Vivi's back, indicating with his hands the quacking gesture for talk, talk, talk. That he should thrive throughout lunch on her attention, only to mock her now, diminished him in my eyes, at the same time as he made me his accomplice. I decided to distance myself from them both.

The next day, Vivi wanted to return to the same restaurant. I said I did not like to repeat experiences, so Branko and Vivi dined that day alone. On the bus back to Siena, Branko surprised me by taking the seat at my side. He told me Vivi had a terrible earache; they had tried to phone some international alert, for which her husband had bought insurance, and failing any contact, he had suggested that Vivi sit down and relax and eat something first, and when she swallowed her soup, the

thing blocking her inner ear seemed to burst and the pain
dissolved, after which she felt fine. I thought Vivi's illness a
ploy, and was amazed that Branko had bought it.

Professor Lucke: "Monterchi, a graveyard chapel, circa 1445.
Piero della Francesca. Here we have a tent motif, opened to
the side by angels in a ceremonial way, so that we see the
Madonna del Parto. This is not a common topic in Christian
iconography—the pregnant Mary. You see the swelling of
her body, hidden beneath a blue gown. Her feet are clearly
visible. She turns slightly away from us. Her left hand on her
haunch. Her right hand lies over a slit in her gown, a very
soft, cautious touch; at the same time a gesture, which seems
to point. This is a woman in every sense of the word, expecting. Inside surface—padding—inside of a fur coat. Outside a
mantle. Promise of birth. Christ on the cross, promise of res-
urrection. Location, above the altar in a chapel of a graveyard.
The meaning of the Eucharist. She is the chalice that carries
the Lord. Like the tent that shelters her, her gown shelters her
body, her body shelters Him. Pomegranate. Eucharistic sym-
bol. Round and opened like her gown." Professor Lucke is
excited as he points, his fingers flying here and there, dancing
in his running shoes, his eyes on fire with the symbols on the
wall. His loose cotton shirt billows like the wings of an angel
as the sweat blossoms under each arm, with its pungent male
odour, prompting Eva to comment, "He wants a woman," not
in the carnal sense, but in the sense of a man wanting a
woman to administer to the details, such as laundering his
shirts.

I usually spent my weekends in Siena with Eva, lounging beside the *Giardino* pool. With Eva, there were no expectations, not even the necessity of conversation. We would sit side by side on our lawn chairs, observing the bathers from other countries over our respective books, in parallel pursuit. Eva studied the course books in preparation for our final exam, while I read Boccacio. Thus, in silent companionship, our eyes filled with the same images: There was this Swedish girl in a loose white bathing suit, draped off her small breasts with their dripping nipples, perched with a single bronzed foot coyly fishing the pool. Her young muscular mate swam up to her, lifted the foot from the water and, astonishingly, sucked her toe.

"Isn't she gorgeous?" was Eva's singular comment, admiring the human animal which she had nursed in all its extremities. Eva was of an age—beyond surprise, beyond longing, accepting of seemingly everything. That day, and although Eva and I usually practised our student economies, we ate at the *Giardino* restaurant. Without changing out of my black bathing suit, I simply wrapped Vivi's scarf about my waist and waited in queenly composure for the barbequed lamb to be brought to our table, treating Eva to wine. When supper was ended, I could not leave the bones on my plate. Wrapping them carefully in a napkin, I deposited them into my beach bag. Eva said nothing. Later, we laughed like complicit schoolgirls over the contemptuous silence of our Sienese waiter, removing my boneless plate. In the privacy of my cell-like room back at the *Conservatori,* I gnawed again upon my bones, with a hunger beyond need.

While I usually spent my weekends with Eva, one weekend I went to meet Vivi in Bologna. Our purpose was shopping. Vivi was taking me in hand. If I were to become a lawyer, I must dress the part. In Bologna, I would find Armani suits and Bruno Magli shoes. Vivi knew just the right stores, and there was a hotel across from the train station where we would each take a room.

I arrived before Vivi. Though discussed weeks before, we had not confirmed with each other before the designated weekend, so I was uncertain if she would, in fact, keep to the arrangement. Was it for this reason or some other that I made all my purchases without her? In the shoe store where I selected my shoes and bag, I told the saleswoman I would be practising law on my return to Canada. "In these," she told me, "the judges will not be able to resist your persuasions." For the black Armani suit, with buttons up the left side of the skirt, I would find a handmade white-and-black shirt. I made my choices in an orgy of spending, all in one morning. Surrounded by a sea of tissue paper on the floor of my hotel room, I surveyed the purchases for which Vivi's approval had not been sought, and a wave of nausea overcame me. Was it the extravagance of what I had just done, or fear of my own choices?

At dinner, I told Vivi that I had been about to leave Bologna after my purchases, uncertain of her arrival. She burst into tears. Tonight was her birthday. I could not possibly have known…to have been abandoned by an alcoholic mother, a father unable to care for her, being given into foster care. She had grown up thinking of the children who came and went as her brothers or sisters, never to see them again, never knowing when they would disappear. Her father had thought he could get her back, had apparently tried—a fact not known to Vivi until the year after his death, when she had traced her birth parents and learned for the first time that she had been wanted by at least one of her life givers, that her father had tried. He had thought the child custody order temporary, not appreciating how in legal terms temporary can become final. There was one birthday when a man arrived at the door. She was sent to her room, but not before she saw the shadow of his form, the doll in his hands. They were delicate hands, with long aesthetic fingers—the hands of a pianist or an artist. The doll had a porcelain head, later broken by one of Vivi's foster brothers. Now Vivi had a vast collection of dolls at her home back in Canada, the one built for her by her German husband. She had four sons of her own. No, I could not imagine the sense of abandonment had I not been there in Bologna.

"Duccio: We look into an interior, into something that could be part of a larger structure. Time here is convincing. People are joined together, having a meal—drinking, eating, talking, but lively. There is one in the centre. Again we have the motif of the one who leans against him. For sure, these people spoke Italian. We seem to hear them. Notice how much Duccio operates with hands, in contrast to Giotto, who seems even to hide hands. When shown at all, Giotto's hands are at rest. In Duccio, in proper perspective, the lines should converge on Christ. That would recess him. The way it is here, in the Duccio, the convergence point is outside the back wall. What principles did these people operate with? There is a construction, a syntax, an order that brings the disparate parts into a whole. These splinters of perspective—are they renderings of observation or constructions unidentified with external sight? We can't see this painting from Renaissance eyes. This is a way of seeing the world unknowable to modern eyes."

In Assisi, we dine together—Branko, Vivi, Professor Lucke, and I—a rare night together, never to be repeated. Eva is bedridden, having eaten some tainted food. She takes her incontinence as a sign of demise, apologizes when I surprise her, weeping alone in the dark when I return with some tea. I had thought Eva beyond grieving, not understanding that one can always grieve one's own life. Eva, then, had been *afraid*. Alone in the darkness of our cave-like room in Assisi, Eva had been afraid.

That day, in Assisi, we learned of the Franciscans. "In the Franciscan spirit, there is the discovery of the individual, who has the capacity to judge, who in a sense needs to be converted." Like Professor Lucke himself, whose deepest need is to be converted—to believe. It is easy for those who do, impossible for those who cannot. Faith cannot be willed. Like love. Neither for him, nor for me. "God is perfect. Man is imperfect. Whatever is imperfect cannot be God. But Christ was born man. Yet he was a spiritual being, was not man. This must have been a deadly challenge to the Church, this Christian paradox. It meant in his very core God was man, born man, became man, lived like man, died like man."

Professor Lucke, Branko, Vivi, and I eat together in an outdoor garden of arbours and vines. A guitarist from the nearby campground plays Neapolitan love songs. At outdoor kitchens carved into caves, there are large open hearths; we select our meals at the cave mouths. I have quail on a spit, cooked peppers, and rapini. We bring Professor Lucke his favourite pasta, *con oglio e aiglio*. And, of course, there is the wine!

In the arboured garden, our separate realities seem to coalesce. We draw near. Professor Lucke confesses to the problems of teaching in Italy, how he can see some people are coping with so much other than the course — it may be a bug in the bathroom or something else. People are overwrought because everything is different. We begin talking about opera and intense experience when Branko repeats the Tosca story I heard in Rome about the transposition in the music signalling some epiphany in the plot. Professor Lucke tells Branko he likes opera because the music distances the emotion. He has this abstract thing to contemplate, interposed between himself and raw emotion. Vivi says it is only deep experience that make life worth living. I sit distant and silent, wrapped in the scarf. My silence is wilful, for Branko has told me that afternoon I am too caught in the vortex of myself, that I do not see people around me — the way they move away, as if from a fire, realizing that I know exactly what I want and, my God, I'm going to get it, and they had better get out of my way until I'm done. "You are hard to be with."

Vivi tries to capture Professor Lucke's attention the whole evening. Then, unexpectedly, Professor Lucke leans across the table and says into my silence: "This is a beautiful scarf." His thumb catches the fabric, like the scene of the lamentation with St. Francis outstretched, *and Girolomo, the one who could not believe, he catches the fabric and pulls it up and free of the wound and then pushes his fingers into it. We see him do that with terrific concentration. We see him from the back kneel down in businesslike fashion. "I want to know,"* in contrast to everyone else, *whose response is raw emotion.* Professor Lucke brings his face close to the scarf, and I can smell the sweat rise from his unwashed body. Vivi smiles triumphantly, taking the compliment as her own, but says nothing to betray me. She and I alone know that I would not have bought it but for her. It is her taste he compliments, but *I* am the scarf. It is my beauty he means. I am beautiful—for the first time in my life.

Toward the end of the evening, the others start asking Professor Lucke about art. I say our conversation will become too much like work. Professor Lucke says, "My God, you *know* me." Then, "We have four weeks still to go." We have come too close, too fast. In fact, we will never again break bread together with Professor Lucke after that. *For not much longer now will I be with you.*

The next day, on a street in Assisi, he and I pass each other alone. Professor Lucke says he wanted to thank me for my company. He was sorry he hadn't the chance to talk with me, but he was distracted by the full conversation on his other side. "You," he says, "are very independent. One can see that immediately. Often independent people drive away what they need."

Donatello's "The Conception": "'Yes, I will be the hand-maid of the Lord,' and the very minute she gives her assent, she conceives. She hasn't here yet given her assent. Donatello focuses in on that moment, and gives it to us with a kind of dynamism. She doesn't say 'no'; she says 'yes,' but the concep-tion takes place only when she says 'yes.' In this mural, it has not happened yet. This is the moment *before choice*."

Never, for a moment, conceiving there could be far worse…

When they put you in my arms and I looked into your face at those eyes, wide-open and searching for me, I, who had heard your first cry, who could not stop crying, had heard that tall ships, passing before the mouths of caves at the very moment sun entered, as through a shutter, left a negative of the ship on the back of the cave; thus you were imprinted upon me, your face like a negative upon my mental plate.

"Momma, how will I bear it?" I went to your father's apartment to tuck you in during those first nights of our sep-aration. In the bathroom, I washed your little face, contorted with pain, watched you square your little shoulders, and go out to face your fear. *You will bear it because you must, because you have no choice. I did this to you.*

"She stares at her baby Jesus and sees right into his future. She says 'yes' to conception, knowing of His impending sacrifice."

It takes me over twenty years to understand the gift of Vivi's scarf. By then a middle-aged woman with only one son to my flesh, I have an afternoon of love. I have emerged damaged but not broken from a failed marriage. To my surprise, there is a man in my life, enough years my junior to make me remember Eva. Remembering Eva, *I do not refuse*. We have all we can expect—a few hours on a Sunday afternoon between our respective obligations, the children's hockey games, their birthday parties. How shall I greet you? Wear nothing, he says, we haven't much time. But I cannot bring myself to open my door naked. It is not the fear of nakedness, but of my own imperfection—that he will see the unholy blemishes of this sacred temple, the Caesarean section, the imperfections of a life half used.

Vivi, I wrap myself in a vortex of colour. I stand behind my front door, a woman, in every sense of the word, *expecting*.

Ah, the delight of his eyes when I open the door, of his hands, searching the colourful folds for an opening. Vivi's scarf is the wrapping. I am the gift.

Vivi will return that summer after Florence to find a different colour of hair in her own hairbrush, left in the lavish master bathroom of her perfect home, while she went to Florence to study art. Is it always thus we discover ourselves betrayed? What choice did she have? The choice only of reaction. I was not there to witness. I will remember Vivi as one moment— the moment she threw the scarf in all its colours about herself under the Florentine sun. *If you don't, I will*.

Vivi, I wrap myself in the vortex of colour. I do this in memory of you.

the caller

I KEPT HER number in my purse, in the slot reserved for mirrors. Whenever I was on a bus or sitting at a lunch counter and had nothing to do, I would take out the number and contemplate it. How strange it would be, I thought, if anything happens to me. The police will go through my purse. They will find my name and this phone number. They will call her, thinking me a friend, someone she knows.

"Muir?" she will say, "I've never heard of any Muir." I worried about this. I worried about the police giving her trouble.

Why did I keep it, then, when I had it committed to heart anyway? Perhaps because of the way it came to me — out of air, out of nowhere, on a night I could not sleep.

I was having a cup of tea. I thought I would go through my purse and see what I could find. I found a lot of old bus transfers and a dusty pen.

It was then that the mystery happened. I was testing the pen on one of the old transfers. Before I knew it, I had written down seven numbers. Where did they come from? I must try the number and see if I recognized the voice.

She came to the phone out of breath. I imagined her running into this room from another. There were voices in that other room. I tried to hear what they said, but couldn't make out the words above the music. And then a man's voice called to her. "Who is it?"

There was a pause. She did not answer. She was listening to me. "Who is it?" he called again, sounding irritated, wanting her back with him, with their friends.

"No one," she said briskly, and hung up. It was like the toss of a head, her hanging up.

I hung up too.

My kitchen felt very quiet after that. I went back to the cup of tea. It had gone cold. I hadn't bothered to turn on a light. I never do at night. I usually sit with only the night light. I like the way its soft yellow glows across the plastic tablecloth, reminding me, somehow, of Christmas. But tonight, it was not at all comforting. I wished for someone to be there with me. The voices had filled me with a nameless longing; they had banished sleep.

She had listened. She had not hung up. That was the strange thing. Was she waiting for someone to call? Someone in particular? I wondered why a voice like hers, a young voice with other voices waiting in the background, would listen alone in the dark? I saw her in the cool dark of a bedroom, with winter coats piled on the bed. I saw her standing there, the phone held in her hand, eyes meeting her own eyes in a mirror.

I did not use the number again for a long time after that.

I was afraid that if I used it too often she would have it changed. So I spread out the calls, sometimes not calling for weeks. In my mind, I would note the date of each call, and be proud of the time I'd placed in between — days I'd managed to live through alone, without needing another soul on earth.

Then her hours changed. She surprised me by answering during the day. The day used to be my way of delaying a real call. I would imagine the phone ringing through her empty rooms, connecting me to her. While she was out, I would run my fingers across her furniture, open cupboards and drawers. But she was at home. The next week, too, she was at home. What did she do for a living? The man whose voice I had heard at the party never answered. She was the only one who ever did. It was her phone, then. She could be almost any-thing — a painter, a nurse, a student — but someone who keeps strange hours. She lived alone.

Late one night, she answered on the first ring. Her voice was dream-heavy. The phone must be near her bed, on the night table. I saw her hand fly out, the reaching instinctive, her voice rose from sleep.

"Hello…."

It took her moments to realize there was not going to be any answer.

"Who is this? Who is on the line?" And then, "Fool," she said.

That surprised me. The way she said it — slow, considered. Not "stupid fool" or "old fool" — just "fool." She was intelli-gent. Of all the crude abuse she might have hurled at me, "fool" was the one word that had come to her mouth. She was awake now. And she had noticed these calls.

I let her hang up on me. I hate to be hung up on, the offensive whine of the dial tone.

I was right to think my calls were not lost on her. I didn't realize that she had set the phone down when the music swelled in my ear. I listened to the music, hardly daring to breathe. It could not have lasted more than a minute. What did she mean by it? What did she want me to understand? Unexpected, like a gift, it seemed to come from some impulse to love, a reckless gesture of tenderness and caring. When the piece was over, she set the phone very carefully back on the hook. I heard the click, and hung up quickly, before I would have to listen to the dial tone. I didn't want anything to break the delicate feeling of the music—so sweet, so sad. Not a word had passed between us.

It was late afternoon when my phone rang, startling me from sleep. No echo of a dream remained. So deep was I in sleep that I had answered several questions before realizing what the call was about.

The market researcher was asking me how likely it was that I, or anyone else in my household, would buy a home computer within the next year? She gave me a range of answers, and I had only to select one to satisfy her question. Very possible, likely, not very likely, not at all. Brisk. Efficient. No time to lose. Racing against my threshold of tolerance. One of the following is your usual brand of beer: Amstel, Labatts, Molson Golden, Molson Export.... I did not drink beer, I finally had to tell her.

The first questions had been easy, requiring a yes or no answer. In this way she had drawn me into the rhythm of question and answer. How hard it is not to answer when one is asked, and when the answer is suggested within a limited range of possibility.

One final question: May I have your name and address, please? Hesitation. No, I told her flatly, I could not give her that. It is only that, she said, they do not believe me if I don't give them a name; they do not believe I really took the survey. Your first name will do, and the nearest intersection to your home. Again, a way of answering had been suggested.

The call was over. I did not mind having been interrupted in sleep. She had given me a key.

What would I, if I had my heart's choice, ask her? The problem was that my questions must all be confined to products. What could I ask about things that would reveal anything?

Do you drink tea or coffee in the morning?

If you had to describe yourself in terms of a smell, would it be animal, vegetable, floral or fruit?

I devised a series of entirely innocent and forgettable questions, based on the shelves of products I viewed weekly on my trips to the Dominion. What a difference it made to have a guiding purpose now behind each selection.

I practised into the silence. I went down the list of faceless questions using the same brisk tone as the market researcher. But when it came to the real call, my tongue froze in my mouth.

"Adam?" she said, "If that's you, please say something." I said nothing. She fell silent. That is, she stopped talking. But I heard this soft little whimper on the other end. I could not leave her like this. I could not hang up while she was crying. So I held on to the phone. Sometime later I heard her blow her nose in another part of the room. She had left the phone off the hook. I heard her run some water from a tap. Minutes later the line was still open.

Our acts have unpredictable consequences — even this smallest gesture of reaching toward another through the phone. I realized she had put a totally different face upon my silence. She thought of a man, a man she thought still cared enough about her to make this tenuous connection. I knew that to maintain silence any longer might harm her. It might cause her to believe in something which, for him anyway, had quite probably ceased to exist. I must do something. With my next call, I could remain silent no longer.

She was polite. She did not hang up on me when I told her I was a market researcher and would like to ask her a few questions.

When I reached the end of my list, I told her that the Marketing Group always made a gift of its products in exchange for her participation. Could I have her address? To my surprise, she agreed. What was the most convenient time to make the delivery? Wednesday afternoon. She would be home around four o'clock.

This threw me into a flurry of preparations.

A trip to the Dominion to purchase the gifts — a bar of soap, detergent, packaged soup, a can of tomato sauce, cookie mix, shampoo, deodorant, tinfoil…. Then I had to find a box of just the right size, and wrapping paper to cover the print. It had been years since I had anyone to whom I could give anything.

I worried about my clothes. Everything in my cupboard seemed inappropriate. There were the dresses I had worn to friends' weddings more than thirty years ago, with matching pillbox hats; my housedresses, and the clothes of my mother's I had kept.

I selected a plain brown suit, which I remembered my mother wearing to work. It was a little heavy for summer, but would have to do.

She lived at the other end of the city. It was a long way to go by public transit. I gave myself several hours. I could arrive early, and freshen up in some coffee shop washroom before hunting for her address.

It was sweltering. Even the air seemed to sweat. I carried the box toward the end of my street, toward the first of the many bus stops I would wait at that afternoon.

The heat had silenced everyone on the bus. The driver seemed to start when I asked him to call out my first street. I tried to rest. A hot breeze blew against my face through a crack in the window. I felt sweat roll down my side from my breast.

During the journey, my sense of time faltered and grew dim. How many changes of bus? How long did I wait at how many corners? At length, I arrived. But standing at the head of her street, I had the strange sensation that I was on my own street again, facing home. The rows of tall houses looked narrow as candles, their rooftops incandescent as lighted wicks.

The heat had baked the day silent. I moved toward her number in a vacuum of silence, as if sealed in a glass jar like some preserve, with all the air and sound boiled out from around me. I would have dropped the box and tried to scream had not the distant sound of a violin reached me. It drew me down the street until I stood outside a house. There were three flights of stairs. When forced to pause for breath at each landing, the music restored me. I knew the melody from somewhere, but was too exhausted to try to remember the source of recollection.

As I mounted each step, I had to struggle against spells of giddiness, and at the same time, a mounting dread. What would I say? What if there was no response? I was too exhausted to return. The thought was inconceivable. Impossible that I should turn around and go away with my gift ungiven. My whole will now strained toward this one and only thing—to place my gift in her hands.

The door opened and I recognized her. That is, I knew her in the way I knew the music, without being able to remember the source.

"Hello," she said.

I could not heave a sound into my throat. I felt my jaw drop open and tremble in an effort to communicate. I squeezed the sweat from my eyes and held out the box. She took it, more I thought to relieve me of the burden than anything else. She looked at me with alarm.

"Here," she said, "Come in. I'll make you a cup of tea."

With the kettle on to boil, she brought me a glass of cold water.

"The stairs," I managed, "the heat…"

She touched my hand and smiled.

"It's all right," she said, "you may rest here."

I looked at her and again felt a start of recognition. After a time she said, "Is there anyone I can call for you?"

"Yes," I said and, on an impulse, I gave her my own number.

She dialled it, and while she waited for someone to answer, she looked at me closely. I looked away.

I was right about one thing anyway. She kept her phone near her bed. Her room, in fact, was very much like my own — a bed sitting room, with a single cot against the wall, a floral cover for the daytime to make it look like a couch. Was it possible she lived like me, was even as lonely?

At length she placed the receiver back on the cradle.

"Who are you?" she said finally. "Who, really, are you?"

I hesitated. I stood up and went toward the door. At the same time she stood up and went toward the door, as if to prevent my escape.

"Perhaps," I said slowly, turning to look upon her a last time, "perhaps I am no more than a possibility of you, which you must do everything possible in your life to avoid becoming."

I fled the room. I have no recollection of the journey home, a journey that took me back across the city. But when I arrived, my phone was ringing. I went to it and lifted the receiver.

"Hello?" I said.

There was no answer.

a promise to noma miller

> April is the cruellest month, breeding
> Lilacs out of the dead land, mixing
> Memory and desire, stirring
> *Dull roots with spring rain*
>
> "The Waste Land," T.S. Eliot

WE'RE SURE HAVING fun out there, aren't we? Yes we sure are. Laughing and joking. I'll bet you thought, who is that crazy woman in the corner making all that noise, just like some empty milk can? I knew what you were thinking. I noticed you, sitting over there with your back to me, just the way my mother used to sit over her knitting, pretending she heard nothing, but she heard everything. I knew you were listening. I just knew. It was meant to happen tonight. Fate strikes in the washroom. Anyway, you know what I said to them? They're all laughing out there at me. I says…shush now, let me think. I can't think right when there's noise. I says, I put the cows in the…wait now, I'll get it right. I put the cows in the silo, I milked the chickens, and I put the pigs out to pasture. No, I'm no farmer hick from around here. I'm an actress. Don't you get it? I put the cows in the silo, I milked the chickens, and put the pigs out to pasture. Farmer she says! You from around here? You're not from around here. I could tell the minute you walked in. Soon as I heard your voice, I knew you weren't from Beeton. Beeton, named after the bees, only they don't have no bee farms here anymore. I'm from Toronto too. But I've been everywhere in the world. Just everywhere. I'm an actress. You've got to go wherever there's a job. You live for them lines, those words that don't live until you speak them.

Would you listen to that! Well, would you listen to that! Actresses lie, she says. But I'm telling the truth. You can believe me. Hush. Hush. Shush now. You can't tell anyone. Promise me now. No one around here knows. You see, I'm retired now. I don't act anymore because I can't hold the lines together. They all slip away, blow away like the way the wind spreads newspaper pages in the streets.

Oh sure, go ahead. That one doesn't flush. I'll just wait for you here beside the sink and comb out this mess. Now where did that lipstick tube get to? I used to have such thick black hair when I was your age. After the accident, it all fell out in handfuls. It got so as I was afraid to brush it. Noma, Noma, you're a mess. Why just look at you.

I live here now in an apartment for senior citizens. Now, I won't hear of you telling me lies, telling me I don't look that old. I didn't hear a thing…. Oh…. No, not an old folks' home! They don't let you do anything in them places. I can take care of myself. I got a nice little place with a bed-room and a living room and a kitchen. It's cheaper that way.

I'm retired now. So, what brings you to the Beetonia Hotel? How many acres you got? Now where exactly is it? About eight miles east out of town, over the bridge, beside the old graveyard. You mean the one where the Methodist church burned? I know the place. The little shack on the corner. Renting it, eh? You know, I used to write too. You've got to have quiet. You just can't have any noise. I always used to tell my mother I just couldn't think with all that noise. She'd just keep banging those pots, just like she hadn't heard me asking, like she never wanted me to be anything. You've got to have someone who believes in you and what you're doing to make it seem real. My mother always used to make it silly, like those things weren't important in life. Nothing was important but work and whether you ate. Writing wasn't work to her. How can somebody you know is stupid make you feel ashamed of what you believe in? Anyway, life's humiliating enough without aching your heart out to put your private thoughts on paper so as they can be ridiculed. You know what I mean.

"That's not life," she says to me. Then she smiles at me and tells me to come by the barn that afternoon and look through the window. "Look deep," she says, "into the dark. Wait till your eyes open in the shadows and you'll see it—all you need to know. It's time," she says, "before you go filling your head with those foolish fancies. What do you think you bleed for every month?" she says to me. I wasn't going to look. I didn't want to owe anything I learned to her. I kept circling the barn, passing the window, and not looking in. I swore I wasn't going to. Then at dinner she kept trying to fix me with those hard grey eyes of hers and smiling like we had a secret now between us. But I wouldn't look at her. I couldn't look at her without seeing it. It made the food stick in my throat and when she saw me leaning over the porch, she laughed. She laughed at me. "That's how it's done," she says to me, "and that's why we're here."

What are you thinking? Why shouldn't I tell you my secrets? Use them for what? What do you mean never mind? You're awfully silent for someone who works with words....

Sure, what do you think I've been standing here for? We'll go out together as soon as you wash. That tap is kind of rusty. The water comes out red.

So you'll be here the whole summer, eh, all by yourself? Just what are you going to do with yourself and four walls for the whole summer? You can't write all the time. Walk? Well, what do you want to walk for? There isn't anything to write about around here. C'mon, dry your hands and we'll go out together. Take your time, I'll wait for you....

Well, I'd be delighted to. My nerves are kind of bad tonight. I need some company. Beer, thank you. Hey, Bill, she's from Toronto too. What are you looking so down in the mouth about? She's inviting me, Noma, to a drink. And you see, Bill, we aren't all crazy from Toronto after all. But I don't want to sit over there. She asked me! Don't pay any attention to him. Don't listen to a word he says about me. Would you look at this place. "Please refrain from using obscenities." "No gambling after twelve o'clock." "No minors." "Keep shoes on while dancing." You ever seen such a place? You know what he says to me the other day? He says running this hotel was like teaching grade school, he says, you've got to put coats on and send us home. You've got to tell us what to do and keep us from ruining each other's pleasure. He wants to make us all sit in our corners and keep our mouths shut, just so as we'll drink more, sit like a pile of pigeons on a fence. Well, there aren't enough corners, Bill. It's a morgue you're running, a morgue. Pumping us up with preservatives and sending us off pickled.

What did you say your name was? I'm Noma Miller. Guess what I'm thinking. Go on, guess. I'm thinking how much you remind me of me when I was young. I used to be beautiful like you. Of course, you wouldn't know to see me now. My hair is a sight. Oh, go on. I get it done, you know, once a week, only I go tomorrow so that's why it's such a mess. I knew when I heard your voice. Just like it was meant to happen tonight. Fate strikes in the washroom. Now you tell me what you're going to be and I'll tell you if you should or not. Go ahead, tell me what you're going to be. Writer, that's it, that's a good life. That's better than acting. You can't act without the words. You've got to have them words. You know, when I was young I wrote. I wrote a book. My sister, she says to me once, whatever did happen to that woman? Did she marry him, she says to me? I ripped it up, I says. What did you go and do that for, she says? I tore it up. You've got to have someone driving you. You see, when I was acting, I got to thinking how good the words were and I was ashamed of my own. My brother, he was nine, he asked me, too. I says, how did you know about that? Because I read it, he says, got it down from your shelf.

Then there was this man who ran a little newspaper. He hears of this story he wants me to cover. Anyway, I goes and writes a by-line for him. And my mother gets a hold of it and reads it, and she says to me, "What are you trying to be, Noma? You can't be no reporter, no journalist. You aren't good enough." So I took that story and I ripped it in front of her face, slowly like, right in front of her face, like it was her I was… She banged that kitchen door, so's you could hear it clean out to the barn. You've got to have quiet. You've got to be alone with just you and your imagination. You know that, don't you?

"Writer," she says, "you little barn brat?" It's not ugly, being alive, I kept telling myself. I had secrets too. Only she could see deep, she could, and without saying a word she'd lay everything flat like a hay field after a bad rain. And what she couldn't guess I'd tell her. Something senseless made me do it every time, like I had to, almost like I wanted to. Like I felt I deserved it. Then, after she had shamed me, I'd feel free, not guilty anymore and that was my biggest secret — that hating her kept me from hating myself. She never knew that — never — how, when I got that way, she couldn't hurt me any-more. I'll tell you, though, I get the queerest feeling some-times and it makes me kind of desperate. You see, hate eats up too much energy and I sometimes think she's still laughing at me.

Soon as I heard your voice, I just knew tonight…. My horoscope told me I was going to meet this special person who was going to change my whole life. I'm Sagittarius. Pisces? Why we're the worst, most awful possible combination imaginable. We could destroy each other. I won't answer another question, not another one. I'm the one who drives you. Seeing you there, looking so young and strong…. You can't drive me, you're a Pisces…. I almost have a wish…but it's too late. You aren't going to try and make me be something. It's too late. But if you were mine, I'd drive you to the edge of hell. I'd never let you ruin yourself or cheat one drop of talent, I wouldn't. I'd wring you until you were dry, I'd make you….

What was that you called me? Amanda. Why, wherever did you get the idea my name was Amanda? A character from what play? I was educated once, you know. I know what you're talking about. Touch me. Go on, touch me. That's my hand you're touching, something you'll never find on the printed page. Me, Noma Miller. I'll tell you something about words you've got to know so as you'll respect some things and not go thinking about every experience, every bit of joy and suffering as something you can use. Before you make a word, the thing you want to make it for is all fluttery and strange, missing something, a way to understand it maybe, and for an instant you want to leave it and not talk about it because it doesn't need you. Then you name it and try to make it your own and like loving or hating, you take something away, but there's always something else you can't name, something you can't quite have. Like the time I was standing by myself in the woods near the farmhouse and the wind rose and the trees lifted their dark branches and I thought of a bride rustling in her silk nightdress and I was going to write it down, my thought, because it seemed even more beautiful than the trees and then I knew I ruined my moment because I had thought about it and it wasn't the same anymore. So I put it away like you put something in a drawer you might use someday but never do, and it made me feel sad and kind of powerless. And now I've given it to you. But you can't ever know what it's really like when the trees lift their branches at night as if a bride let slip her silk nightdress and came whispering to her lover.

Never name anything you can't change without regret. It's a sad life you've chosen and cruel too. Because there are things you'll write about that you never should have, and things you'll find you made smaller than they really were. I'll tell you something maybe I shouldn't say. I'm afraid of you. The way you sit there looking at me — so calm, unmoved. Nothing I say really means anything to you for what it says, and all the time I know your mind is working. You're here pretending you're listening, but I know that you're listening to something else, deep inside yourself, your own voice, composing. You see? There you go again, looking amused, just as if you like hearing even yourself uncovered. Makes you feel naked, doesn't it? Kind of helpless to have someone know you. You can't hide your look behind that glass and your trying to only makes it obvious. You're to take what I'm saying seriously. I'm a little afraid of you, because I know…I know I can't keep my thoughts together, or keep myself from looking ridiculous. But you can, if you cared to. You can do anything with words.

Anyway, it's Noma, Noma Miller. There was this director, and he says to me "Noma Miller? Why that's easy to remem-

[147]

ber—that's a perfect name." Noma, as in lightbulb, you know? Noma light bulbs, and Miller, like the little moths that fly to the light, the moths that stick to the light bulbs and burn their little wings. Millers are moths. What do you mean you never heard of it? It's an old Canadian word. Sure you heard of millers. Well, I'll tell you, you just go and take your lamp into the woods this summer, and stand there for a while and every insect in the forest will come to you. They'll come and knock their senseless little heads against that glass like they wanted in, just like they wanted to die, and you'll see the most beautiful millers you'd ever want to see, millers with white wings and little red eyes tapping the glass. Big black moths with streaks, swinging around the lamp and dusting their miller powder all over the glass where they tap like little powder puffs. If you stand near the lamp you'll feel them fluttering past you, brushing your face just like they were lonely souls stroking the night for something friendly.

Say, why don't you and me write together? We'll sit in the same room, you with your empty paper and me with mine, and we'll make something out of all the secrets we have locked in here. We'll share what's before you and still possible, and what's behind me and done. We'll make something whole out of all the little pieces.

I knew just as soon as you walked in that we'd be friends. I'm having the time of my life. You know, I haven't been so happy in all my life. My nephew'd never believe me. He'd never believe that I'm sitting here with you. He's my heir you know. Comes to visit me sometimes. I got a real nice place. Say, you could stay there with me. Do you have hay fever?

Well isn't that lucky. You can take my bedroom…. See, I have hay fever and this time of year with the wind blowing around all the new weeds, cattails, and dandelions, I just can't stand the bedroom—faces a farm. You take my bedroom and I'll sleep in the living room. Now really, I mean it. Sure I mean it. I've got you now. I'm never going to let you go. You're mine now. I'll drive you to the edge of hell, I will, and you'll write for me. You will. I'll give you my ideas.

I never had anyone. That cruel stupidity of hers, reducing everything to something dark, heaving, and struggling in the hay, in a dung-filled barn, a moment's dumb desire nothing can ever take back. Here I am—Noma Miller—here because of some selfish, unthinking moment. Anything I say or do can never take away the stupidity of my own beginning.

I'm telling you because you're a woman and you know what it's like—how humiliating it can be. Why don't you say something? What are you thinking? Just now, you remind me of her. I remember her standing there beside the stove, heating the oil, and never once looking at me. I just took my piece of paper and I held it in front of her face and ripped it slowly. I ripped it in two and then in little pieces. Maybe having made a thing gives you the right to ruin it. I can't write anymore. Can't hold the thoughts anymore…the words just keep blowing around in there like the way withered leaves collect around your feet in the fall and blow down alleyways. You've got to have quiet. Shush, shush, I kept saying to her. My sister and brother, she was twelve and he was nine, they knew I had to have quiet up there in my room. I had to have

silence so I could make my own words and not what came
out ugly from her mouth. Why'd you go and do that, they
said. I grew so angry at her destroying me inside. I had a
thought, looking at her closed face, so tight it was with its
own hard pride. Then I thought I'd make it so that they
wouldn't come so eager to the barn anymore. And I felt my
hand go out to the fry pan. And then she looked at me, startled like, and we both knew the same thought. I saw what she
looked like afraid and I didn't want to any more. A cornered,
bright-eyed animal — that's what she looked like — until I put
down the pan. Then her face changed, twisted around the
mouth into a kind of smirk, and her eyes were full of hate as
hot as the oil. And I knew she must be seeing the same hate
burning in my eyes. The pan was down. But she knew, she
knew what she never knew before, that I was capable of
doing it, if I'd wanted to. Only, once something like that is
known, you can't ever, ever unknow it. I should have known
her spite wouldn't wait.

After I went up to my room, I couldn't write another
thing. That day I felt as though all my thoughts were emptied
out on the wind and going away from me like the fields in
spring blowing with seeds. Only nothing of me ever grew.

I was looking out at the fields and pretending that life
hadn't been made that way in the dark. I could hear their
baby voices so full of the moment. They were playing in the
yard. After that everything went all fluttery, like the millers
and when they asked how it happened, me down there with
my head near split open all over the garden, nobody knew
how it had happened. I couldn't say for sure, what with the

clouds blowing in the sky and everything drowned in the sun, whether I'd really seen someone move away from my window, or saw that hand let my curtain drop. Then there was her face bent over mine. Our eyes met again like before, just before it all went black. I can't say for sure…. You got to have quiet. You got to keep the thoughts all flowing together in a line instead of rising like bubbles in a hot fry pan.

Wait, you can't go now. Stay with me. Just when I found you. You've got to write to me. Stay a little longer. Speak to me. You haven't told me anything about yourself. Wait now — I got a pencil — write and tell me when you're coming again. Let me think. I can't remember…. Here, I've got an envelope my sister sent me a letter in. There's my address there. Now remember, Miss Noma Miller. You can just phone information. There's where you write. Look, call me, you promise? Promise you'll write Noma Miller. I'll be waiting for you. Don't forget your promise. I'll be waiting for you to write.

royal pardons

THE BUS LEAVES from Paris. It is just about to leave when a man arrives, all in a flap. "Is this where you get the bus for the Loire tour?" Yes, the passengers from that side of the bus tell him. "Oh, thank God. I thought I would miss it." Francesca leans over her mother to get a better look at the last passenger. When names are exchanged, they learn his name is Royal.

First Night in Angais

Francesca washes out their nylons and underwear and takes the first bath. Then her mother takes her bath and comes back into the room, all wrapped in towels, and sits on the bed to complete the day's diary entry. In Paris, mother and daughter have roughed it, living in a dingy old hotel that allegedly housed members of the French underground during the Second World War. They have sponge-bathed from the single sink. "Your father would never keep me in a place like this," her mother pronounced upon seeing Maurice Ballitrand's dank establishment. "Get used to it," fired back Francesca, who controled the holiday purse strings on her meagre copyeditor's salary. "I'm not Dad." At dinner this night in Angais, the "Queen Mother," as Francesca has come to think of one particularly critical female passenger, commented upon their rooms as "passable." Francesca's mother pressed her foot meaningfully under the table. This night of their first bath in a week, Francesca wanted to ask her mother to scrub her back, but a sense of shyness, at twenty-eight, in front of the mother who once wiped and diapered her bare bottom, prevented her.

Now, wrapped in towels, her mother is bent over the page like a sedulous student, writing in the travel diary Francesca gave her on the plane. This trip, too, is a kind of gift — Francesca's gift to herself for having survived her "bad year." It is, as well, a gift of thanks to her mother.

Francesca has taken the bed nearest the window, where she lays sprawled after the day of sightseeing. Her hair, just washed, is spread out over the towel she has neatly placed across the pillow. It is long hair; the ends touch the headboard. She tries not to move her head, luxuriating in this moment of staying completely still — something she could not have achieved a year ago, when she was blown apart from inside, all the pieces flying about.

"How do you spell *croissant*?" her mother asks, biting the rubber on her pencil. Something about the way she pronounces it — quassant — makes Francesca think of the spread of a duck before it lays an egg. Francesca spells *croissant*.

The incident with the washroom and *croissants:* Francesca ordered them both *croissants* as she dashed through the restaurant to the washroom, graciously letting her mother use the washroom first, then pounded on the door with impatience when her mother took too long. Of course, her mother will not write that. Ever forgiving, she will write what they have eaten there, not what occurred. Francesca asks how her mother will remember one place from another unless she attaches something of her own to it, some personal memory: "Like what you told me the other day about Paris always having a wind blowing through it — that's something you noticed."

So when it comes to writing the next day's entry, her mother asks her, what was it I noticed about Paris? And Francesca reminds her about the wind, and Francesca's mother writes an unrelated addendum to that day on the Loire, "And Paris always has a wind blowing through it."

Francesca loves her mother, reading the journal that night while her mother is taking a bath. While Francesca has lain sprawled upon beds all over France, unable to write, her mother has bent over her pages, asking the spellings of place names and writing them down, asking what they have seen that day and where they have been, writing that down as Francesca dictates, "and then we saw…and after that," not realizing her mother writes that down too — her connectives — and always ending with that good night to Francesca's father: "Paris is so romantic, Johnny. I love you so much. Some day we must see this together." All Francesca can manage is a cryptic code. "Marie Antoinette made a note with a needle, the person she was seeking to save her already severed." And her ongoing book of accounts:

Perrier, waiting for tour	13.80 francs
Comédie française, billets	42 francs
Postcards	12 francs
Bread	1.5 francs
Gift, Dad	160 francs
Perfume	87 francs....

On the bus, Francesca stares out the window, just staring at the Loire, the beautiful Loire, with its glittering surfaces, dazzled into somnolence.

Somewhere in Normandy

Royal lights another cigarette. Francesca and Royal are the only two still awake on the bus after a heavy Normandy lunch and too much wine. The tour guide has turned off her microphone and gone to sleep.

Francesca moves across the aisle so as not to disturb her sleeping mother. Moisture lies on her mother's forehead and temples and between her breasts like heavy dew. Her arms are spread slightly to free the underarms and bent at the elbows, like moulted wings. Her mouth emits small pucking sounds. Francesca looks at her. Her mother looks so sweet asleep, even her snore exhausted.

Francesca wants to talk to Royal, to finish the conversation begun earlier, sensing the something unresolved in his nature as there is in her own. That is why you take trips, isn't it, at twenty-eight with your mother, something unresolved? She and Royal are the only two on the bus not asleep.

Francesca watches the smoke spiral up from his cigarette. Suddenly he puts his arm across the back of the seat and turns his body half around. "Come, sit beside me," he says and pats the seat. "Let's you and I talk."

Francesca gets up and sits beside him and says, "So what do you want to talk about?"

"Well, if that's the way you feel about it," he says theatrically, "you can go right back to where you were sitting."

Francesca is startled. It is such a frank dismissal.

She says nothing and stays put.

At lunch, surrounded by people, there had been a kind of recognition. Royal and Francesca were discussing whether to order a second bottle of wine when Royal teased Francesca:

"Never mind. I saw the way you quaffed that first glass down. One bottle indeed! You don't fool me."

Given the chance now to really speak, there seems nothing to say.

The "Queen Mother" has awakened and is listening. She looks around and sees them sitting together. She makes a sour face.

Francesca's mother noticed her hatred for Francesca almost the minute they boarded the bus in Paris. "That woman in the black can't stand you," she whispered in Francesca's ear. "You seem to do that—inspire great love, or great hate in people."

"I know," Francesca said, "I can feel it."

Francesca has taken to calling her the "Queen Mother" because of a dream she had forgotten until they drove up to

Chenonceau, a chateau spanning the Cher. *I know this place,* Francesca thought, *I have been here before.*

There were the swallows flying about the high windows of a tower where the "Queen Mother" had entered with her ladies, all in rustling black silk, like ravens, ready to encircle and murder her—a king's wife—for being barren. And the king, arriving just at that moment, held up his arm, a moulted falcon on his wrist, and cast a black shadow across the women who included his own mother. Underneath his cloak, Francesca, who was not Francesca in the dream but the King's barren wife, heard the muffled voices, the distant angry sound, and then felt a rush of wind, followed by the sound of feet, the tower doors closing. After that, he let her go.

Francesca saw the tower, heard the screaming swallows, the same wind caught at her trench coat, and she felt that hate behind her—all in the atmosphere of her dream seven years ago, or four hundred—the very same.

"...Louise de Lorraine," explains the tour guide from Avignon, "the wife of Henry III, had her rooms painted black and white, the colours of court mourning, after the assassination of her husband by Jacques Clement in 1589...." Royal flies about the gallery, touching woodwork and window frames, exclaiming at the view.

"Henry, you remember from the portrait at Azay-le-Rideau, was often portrayed with an earring in his ear. He was the homosexual king. And, in fact, Louise de Lorraine did not bear any children."

"You never know," Royal says in a stage whisper. "They

may have been good friends." The guide winks at him and continues.

"After her husband's death, Louise de Lorraine went into elaborate mourning. All her walls were painted black and her ladies were dressed in black, while Louise de Lorraine appeared all in white."

"How dramatic." Royal claps his hands together and bends his knees slightly, playing to the crowd, "Can you imagine the effect? I love it."

"People are always threatened by the unconventional. I know how people respond to me. I can read their body language," Royal tells Francesca sometime later on the bus.

Francesca is in a washroom combing out her hair when the "Queen Mother" emerges from a cubicle. Francesca sees her sharp look of censure in the mirror when she sees Francesca combing her hair.

"Look how long it is," she exclaims. She has on her black tweed skirt again, a change of blouse, and her sensible walking shoes. Her salt-and-pepper hair is cropped close to the skull with the same efficiency with which she climbed the 300 stairs to the Abbey of Mont St. Michel before anyone else could and pretended not to be winded. Her nostrils are very wide, and the bell dividing them seems raw from some cold sore. Her eyes are black and liquid, giving her a sharp, Jesuitical look. Francesca knows what she is thinking: *A woman of your age should not have long hair, or if she does, should wear it up, confined in a bun.*

"I was just saying to my friend how lovely it is to see a daughter travelling with her mother, taking such good care of her. You're very affectionate with your mother." Francesca can see in the mirror how much the "Queen Mother" despises her.

"You don't look at all like your mother," she says, examining Francesca's face closely. "You'd hardly believe you're related."

"I take after my Dad."

What Francesca cannot see or ever understand is where the hate comes from.

Francesca makes a notation in the little book where she keeps accounts. "There are two women on the tour, alike only in that they wear straight, serviceable skirts with changes of blouse and sensible walking shoes; one made a point of climbing the 300 stairs to Mont St. Michel before anyone else could. She is less feminine than the other—businesslike with chopped-off hair and earth-toned blouses instead of pastels. Her friend wears her hair in a soft French roll and seems more pleasant. There is something deliberate and restless in the first—racing onto the bus so that she can pick a seat away from her friend—something restless as well as nasty. They do not sit together at meals. There seems no reason in their travelling together. The hard one, who I think of as the 'Queen Mother,' speaks of a husband and grown children back home, as if to establish her sex, her usefulness. She does not like me."

Where does the hate come from? It must have something to do with some failure—some transferred anger, a failed relationship, perhaps, with an adult child, reflecting more on herself than on Francesca. What is it she hates? Francesca's love for her mother? Whatever it is, she has to find the worm in the apple, some taint.

Mont St. Michel

The abbey cloister is very delicate with its exposed square of grass and herbs, and breezeway with slender medieval columns. A cool wind blows up the side of the mountain from the ocean. Francesca walks once around with her mother, an arm over her mother's slender shoulders. Francesca tells her mother she has just conceived a desire.

"I want something. I finally want something again."

"What is that?" her mother asks, hopefully.

"A cloister," Francesca announces and laughs hysterically at the outrageousness of her desire. "Just think of it — to be able to walk and walk and walk without ever losing one's way. I'd never be lost again. I love it," Francesca says, spinning round and round, her arms like propellers, all around the cloister, rejoining her mother, out of breath.

Her mother asks carefully if Francesca is any closer to making her decision. She means Francesca's decision about what to do with the rest of her life now that love is dead — whether Francesca will take up that acceptance to law school and accept that she cannot stay the same. *What cannot change dies.*

"I still have time," Francesca says quietly, regaining her composure.

At the base of Mont St. Michel, they wait for the group to come off the mountain. Their bus is parked in the yellow mud of low tide, its wheel marks filled with reflected sky. She stretches out on the concrete breakwater, her head in her mother's lap. The air is golden and smells of salt. She closes her eyes. Incomprehensible tourists' voices in different languages rise and fade. Francesca drifts to sleep.

"What do you really think you'll be doing come September?" her mother asks when she awakens. "In your heart, Franny, you must know."

"You'll be the first to know when I do."

They board the bus.

Clos-Lucé: da Vinci's Last Home

> *Plaise au Seigneur, lumière de toutes*
> *Choses, de m'éclairer, pour*
> *Que je traite dignement*
> *De la lumière.*

Villandry

Outside the gardens of Villandry they have a wine tasting. A long table has been set close to a limestone wall, which glitters in the setting sun. Plates of cookies and overturned glasses hold down the flapping tablecloth. It is like a scene from a Buñuel movie. They emerge from the gardens in clusters of twos and threes and take their places at the long table, basking in reflected light and heat from the wall, all their faces in harmony from the setting sun. Perhaps it is the effect of the gardens, with their splendid proportions and design, or the prospect now of wine, or the harmony of colours in all sunsets. This is the first time they all seem to coalesce: the couple from Mexico in their early forties, arms about each other's waists; then Peter with his movie camera. Everyone on the bus has his or her own mental versions of Peter's movie, watching in fascination as he films the river Cher directly out the side window as they cross a pillared bridge. "Not enough action," Peter says, disappointed, filming a medieval fortress. "Look," encourages their sardonic bus driver, Jacques, pointing to the mouse-hole opening at the fortress base. "Someone has opened a door for you." And they all laugh at poor Peter, who has just gotten over a nervous breakdown, they later learn when he leaves the tour early. He played some part in Hitler's youth, and is ashamed to say he comes from Germany.

Jacques, their bus driver, his black hair slicked back, has already helped himself to a few glasses from the roadside kitchen. "*Ah, les gens,*" he tells the waitress (the waitresses all appear to be in love with Jacques). "*Les gens me font plus mal que mon estomac.*" Pulling up his belt, he tucks his shirt into his pants and walks over to the table.

Royal is demonstrating how the French make champagne. He takes the empty bottle of Vouvray Pétillant and slowly turns it upside down to show how each bottle is siphoned off. The last of the Vouvray dribbles into his glass. Everyone bursts into laughter. "Let me try that, too." The mood of hilarity lasts until dusk. Like shards of glass, briefly they reflect each other's light, brief as glances to a lifetime. By the time they roll back into the bus, the shadows have deepened.

Francesca does not take a picture of that table, of the "Queen Mother" sitting beside Royal, for he has finally charmed even her. Francesca does not want to remember her malevolent smile.

Francesca wants to have a picture of herself and her mother together. She starts to ask Royal, who must think she wants a picture of her mother with him, for he throws an arm around Francesca's mother and poses grandly. At the same instant, he realizes his mistake. ("I was in the theatre once. Some people hate that in me. I sense it instantly....") Through the lens of the camera, her mother's expression is startled and tense. So as not to embarrass Royal, Francesca takes the picture anyway. That night her mother will worry about what her father will think when he sees the photographs developed—the one of this strange man with his arm around her.

"What do you mean, what Dad will think? What should he think? Tell him the truth."

"What truth is that?"

"That Royal is homosexual. The hug was harmless."

"My mother was an ambiguous woman." They are driving back toward Paris, with that heaviness that all returns lay upon the heart. It is as if before they part for good, Royal has to give Francesca this shard of his story. "If she loved my father, she would not show it. The day my father's insurance business folded, she went out and bought a diamond bracelet, as if to say, *If you think I'm going to suffer your failure with you,*

you've got another think coming! Once," Royal remembers, "I
returned home early from school and came up the side of the
house. I caught a glimpse of them through the window. She
was flirting with him outrageously. He was drying the dishes,
and they embraced. They separated the minute they saw me.
I never saw affection pass between them. They hid it from
me. I think that was unfortunate. They didn't know how
comforting it was for me to see that — to know they cared
about each other. I felt very insecure, very doubtful as a boy."

"My parents have always been very affectionate toward
each other," Francesca tells Royal.

"I know," he says, "I can see that."

"… Ate in the town of Chinon. We had the best seat nearest
the window, which Franny grabbed for us. She has taken
good care of me, Johnny. You would be proud of her. We had
a salad, beef, zucchini, and eggplant, and hot peppers and
another salad, and peach Melba with a thick whipped cream.
We must have gained five pounds this holiday. Then we went
on to Azay-le-Rideau, a beautiful castle with water all around
it. Stopped for half an hour at a little town, had a cup of tea,
and a *quassant*."

Royal tells Francesca he once heard Carl Jung speak on television. It must have been twenty years ago. Jung said that
every person has a special destiny. "You may not know what
it is you should be doing, but you know when you are not
doing it because of the level of anguish you feel."

All the failed plays — six of them — and not one of them

ever produced, and the longing to act. To support himself in New York, Royal had worked as a secretary, now with this company, now with that. While in one of these temporary jobs, someone high up in the company noticed him scribbling and put him to work writing a press release. After several years as an insurance underwriter, he woke up one day and realized that he was happy. He realized that he had never been happy while trying to write. Something clicked inside him. He realized that he was doing with his life exactly what he was supposed to be doing, and for the first time, he felt at peace with himself. He only wished his mother could have been alive then to know that he'd arrived, had settled down, so to speak, to know that everything had turned out all right in the end. He was happy. The day he gave up writing failed plays and accepted that he was going to be an insurance underwriter the rest of his life was the happiest day of his life. This trip is one of the fruits of his success—his little gift to himself—for having arrived.

Francesca glances sideways at Royal. He has every right, hasn't he, to indulge himself in this, the Loire Valley tour, in the fruits of his ordinary middle-aged success, enchanted by the glittering surfaces of the Loire, flowing over golden sands in an iridescent shimmer under the pure light of a delicate blue sky? Royal has escaped into his own present. Who can blame him? Who is she to judge? She has no doubt he believes it sincerely, about that day being the happiest day of his life. The day Royal let go of his failed dreams. The day Royal escaped his pain. She thinks it must be the saddest day of anyone's life.

Back in Paris

They will never see each other again. The bus drops off the Loire Valley tourists one by one, Place de La Concorde and then l'Opera, Jean d'Arc, where they lose the "Queen Mother," who bounds off the bus with never a backward glance, charging ahead into the Parisian darkness.

Why should Francesca care? She will never see any one of them again. Except to understand it — the source of the love, the source of the hate. Does it have anything to do with who Francesca really is? Except that the hate can be so damaging, even when disguised as love — especially then.

Louvre. Royal, Francesca, and her mother are the last ones off the bus. Francesca and her mother wander around aimlessly, wondering about going to the bank. They chance into Royal again, who seems equally disoriented. They are momentarily all lost together. And then Royal says, "Come, let's say goodbye properly." He gives Francesca's mother and Francesca a lavish hug. It is a group hug, his great arms flapping around them both. Francesca senses that he is close to tears, but he masks it, as always, in a flourish of drama. She and her mother, laughing out of awkwardness, return the hug, holding Royal against the darkness of that Paris night as he holds them, grateful to each other for the unexpected gift of this embrace.

Francesca and her mother go to a restaurant in the Latin Quarter. Although they have eaten, although neither one of them is hungry, they seek comfort in food.

At the little restaurant on the rue de Buci, Francesca hears herself saying, "How could anyone hate this beautiful city? Adam said he had hated Paris."

It hits them both at the same time. Francesca's mother's eyes become very bright and sparkly.

"When did he say that? Oh, Franny, you didn't call him, did you? Why didn't you tell me?"

"I had to do this all on my own."

There follows a long silence. Mother and daughter have both come perilously close to tears. The room around them feels charged, as if the other diners sense the imminence of grief or an outburst, some exchange of revelations. Or per-haps Francesca and her mother have simply become too used on this holiday to the solitude of language — their little pool of English amid the French diners. The waiter leaves them alone to finish their wine.

"What did you wear?" her mother asks irrelevantly, as she dabs her eyes with the linen napkin embossed with the *fleurs de lis*, which she will later pilfer as a souvenir of this last night in Paris.

"My blue skirt, the one I bought in England, and the white blouse you posted to me in Vancouver."

"Oh, you have prettier things than that." Francesca's moth-er has always believed that no matter how awful you feel inside, you must always "dress for the enemy"; go out to face the world asking yourself: *Who is the person I least want to chance upon today, someone I would never wish to see me at my worst?* and then dress accordingly. During her "bad year," Francesca was barely able to get out of bed, let alone get dressed. That was the year her parents took her back. They sewed the hands back onto her arms, tied the hair back into place, screwed back on the head. Her mother washed and pressed her clothes. They fed her. Somehow she pulled herself together, got herself back to where she had been. But not the same place. Altered. *Damaged*.

"I wore my new spring coat," Francesca adds, "the cashmere coat I got when I came home." Her mother sighs her approval. This makes them both feel better.

"What did he look like?"

"Handsome." Francesca gazes down into her glass. "Handsome, as always."

"What did you talk about?"

"Nothing. Nothing, really. We had nothing left to say. I was even bored. Can you believe it? All these stupid little rituals, like pouring wine from his glass into mine. I looked at him and I thought, was he worth all the suffering? Telling me all the time how much he loved me when really it was hate. No wonder I was confused."

"Franny, ...did he blame us?"

"Who?"

"Your father and me."

"No, he did not blame you," Francesca lies.

"...I wondered where you had gone when I didn't see your name in the magazine anymore. I know how this is going to sound to you, Francesca, but I do care. I do care what happens to you. I need to know you've found some kind of happiness."

"How come?" she asked, her voice sounding more bitter than she had intended. "How come we never worked then?"

Sharp intake of air, then Adam's quick take on it, absolving himself of responsibility. What to figure out had taken Francesca years—had consumed her almost to the point of extinction.

"We were too young, too much in a hurry. We didn't give it enough time…."

And because her question fingered him, now he has to hurt her.

"What are you going to do now, Francesca—I mean with your life?"

"I don't know."

"Well, what are you going to do—just stay at home with your parents? Look at you. You used to act so strong, so purposeful. I used to think: she doesn't know how weak she really is. If anything happens to us, she'll be up her parents' ass."

"I only wish," Francesca's mother starts out of the silence into which Francesca has again fallen.

"What? What do you wish?"

"I only wish you had told me sooner so that it could have been over for me too. Sometimes your Dad and I thought you were still grieving. I only wish he never happened to you."

"Mom," Francesca says finally. "I don't regret Adam. He had to happen. If it weren't Adam, it would have been someone else. He had to be, if I were ever to grow up."

"It didn't have to happen that way. It didn't happen like that for your father and me."

"It was what it was. It's over."

"Is it, Franny? Is anything ever over?"

Francesca does not know this yet. That fall, she will enter law school, embark upon the process of change, of shedding herself like a skin. She will either crop her hair or bind it up in a bun. She is in the process of transforming. Might as well. She can't think of anything better to do. If she cannot create, then at least she will stop breaking her heart and throw herself into this new endeavour—do something that will consume her, that *will burn the hours like fire to human hair. I cannot stay the same, forever still.*

That night in Paris, Francesca's mother gives her a gift.

"You are stronger than I would have been," she says. "You are a strong woman, Francesca."

It is her having called Francesca a woman; it is her believing that Francesca is strong.

Her mother's last entry in the travel diary:

"Had a lovely dinner two doors from our hotel. After dinner walked along the Seine. What a glorious sight—all the lights on the Seine and Notre Dame in the background. What a beautiful place for a couple in love! I'm in love with you, my husband. Some day, Johnny, we will see this together. A beautiful last night in Paris! Francesca has just sorted out all our change. She learns everything so quickly. I forgot to mention that I must have climbed and descended a million stairs this holiday. My feet are so sore."

"For my Mother," Francesca wrote on the inside flap of her mother's travel diary, the one Francesca gave to her mother on the airplane on their way to France together. That trip was a gift—one she could so easily have missed. "For my

Mother — on her first voyage to a feminine city — Paris! May 9th to May 25th, 1980, from your daughter." On the first clean page, Francesca quoted something of herself, something she must have been writing before she stopped writing altogether, confronting the necessity of reinventing herself: "I didn't know where I wanted to be. I didn't want familiarity to reclaim me."

joy, joy,
why do I sing?

THE LOOK ON their dark faces is completely impassive as their uniformed bodies sway with rigid precision from left to right, not the hint of a smile on any of the choristers' faces, in stark contrast to the words they sing. *Joy, joy, why do I sing?*

Her six-year-old son spins out behind the singers Club Med has arranged for its guests this New Year's morning. For his mother's eyes only, he stands poker straight, and then mimics the sway —*Joy, joy, why do I sing?*— the same passive expression on his sun-pink skin. He is himself a choirboy, a reluctant chirper who sang his first Christmas concert just days before their plane embarked on this holiday. Suddenly, she is laughing. Soundlessly, her whole body convulsing with bottled hilarity. Laughing like a schoolgirl. Laughing like she hasn't in years, the tears streaming down her face, hand cupped over her mouth, arm gripping her waist. And her son, seeing this, orbits back. "Did I make you laugh, Momma?" Helpless, soundless laughter, unable to reply, but to nod, up and down. And he is gone again for a repeat performance. The two of them orbiting inside each other's attention, oblivious to the stage, the audience, tuned to each other alone.

A British woman intercepts his next orbit back. She catches the boy firmly by the arm, drags him off to one side. Mother watches as the reprimand unfolds. By the time her son joins her, all the joy has been shamed out of his body. He slumps beside her.

Later that night, when Club Med does its "family" thing and all the staff are on stage, the families dancing and joining in, her son is still crumpled beside her. They sit, side by side, at the very back of the auditorium, behind everyone, out of sight. She spots the British woman, with her two perfect children, cross-legged on the floor before her, clapping their hands, and her perfect husband leaning over to whisper something in her ear. And without knowing how or why, she is down there in front of her, leaning forward with a barely audible whisper.

"I want to thank you."

The British woman looks up and smiles, and then bemused, as the words roll very quietly toward her.

"Right now, my son is at the back of the auditorium, curled up like he has been all day."

The British woman wheels around, sees the little lump, separated by rows of empty seats, from the holidaying crowd. "He was rude. You were encouraging him." Justifications fly up like alarmed birds. These, too, are real. The husband, leaning forward now in alarm, poised to intervene, to come to the wife's defence.

Her voice almost a whisper:

"I can't tell you. I can't make you understand. But you

don't *know*. You just don't know. That's all I wanted to tell you."

At the back of the auditorium, she takes her little boy's hand and squeezes it.

"What did she say, Momma?"

"Nothing. It's fine. Everything is going to be all right. I love you."

"Why don't you ever smile, Momma?"
"I smile."
"No, you don't."

She had been tucking him in when he revealed this to her this past summer before the separation, which occurred in the fall. Those days she had been going from her own busy practice to her father's hospital bed, then to her husband's law practice to pick up his files while he was under suspension from the Law Society, and then home. Every night, she would tuck her boy into bed and crash at his side. Sometimes she slept twenty minutes. Sometimes two hours. When she woke, she'd work the rest of the night at the dining room table. Thinking back, she realizes she probably hadn't smiled in years. Her boy, his eyes trained upon his mother's face, saw everything, saw what she could not allow herself to see.

"Did I make you laugh, Momma?"

He had been giving her a gift. The only gift he could give her that Christmas. A most precious gift. One so rare.

And suddenly she realized why the faces on the Black singers were so deadly serious. Is there anything more serious than joy, the dangerous freedom of singing it out?

Yes, they had been rude. It had been a rude awakening. All realizations are rude. In an instant, commitment to her husband had ended, snuffed out like an ex-communication.

The awful irony is that she had married him for his playfulness, his insouciant, boyish charm.

> *Good morning to you,*
> *We live in a zoo,*
> *With the elephants and the monkeys,*
> *And I love you.*

Thus he had awakened her the first morning after they made love, awakened her with his mock singing. Laughing, she had rolled back into his arms.

In the first year of their relationship, she had this dream: He was holding her under water in a bathtub. He was doing this in jest. Even as she drowned, she knew he did not really mean it. Try as she might to communicate to him the seriousness of her condition, she could not make him understand. He thought the bubbles were playful, the flailing hands, a child's splashing. Finally, she lay perfectly still and tried faking the death she knew was imminent. Still, he did not *get it*.

By late August of the summer of their separation, the headaches were unbearable. She had never suffered from headaches before. Then one weekend, after an uncounted number of extra-strength Tylenol, the pain withdrew to a dull throb. Drawn by the sound of her son and husband's laughter, she went outside, where her boy manned a squirt gun against her husband's hose. She wobbled out toward them. Taking his advantage, her husband ran out to her with the hose, clutched her by the waist, and held the hose directly to her temple. She shrieked in pain as the cold drummed into her head, begging him to stop. Even then, he did not *get it*. She had not yet realized it herself. How he must have hated her to hold her like that. When finally he released her, the headache was back in full force. She threw up in the bushes on her way back to the house.

It isn't personal with him, her senior partner later explained to her. He was commenting upon her husband's financial disasters, which had left so much pain in their wake. "Like a snake, if it's hungry and you're the frog beside it, you'll be eaten. If the reptile's not hungry, it'll leave you alone." She would come to think of it as ice water in his veins — this indifferent passing through time; this not looking backward or forward, not seeing the pain you inflict, *not caring.* Nothing personal. And she also came to realize that, without it, there could never have been any love. How had she missed it? She had been joyless for years.

At Club Med, they announce a family sandcastle-building contest. She and her son go down to the shore with their little Dixie cups, nothing particular in mind. "C'mon, we'll have fun together." She'll work on the moat while her boy stacks towers. They are late for the opening. By the time they arrive at the beach, a Volkswagon convertible has appeared. Two German fathers attack the sand as their children take orders. Holiday transplants with ambition and a plan. They must have known what to expect. This Volkswagon is the product of collaborative design, flawless execution—down to the wheels and sculpted fenders.

She watches in amazement as other sand structures appear—dolphins and giant sea turtles—the product of international families, of the economically secure and highly motivated. She has never seen anything like it—such intense competitiveness over sand. Is it any wonder her son drops his Dixie cup, giving up before they start?

The British woman documents the event through a sophisticated camera and its telephoto lens. Fashion photographer, she wonders, or is the camera simply another private accoutrement of the success everywhere in evidence on this beach, having nothing and everything to do with their real lives? No one here asks what anyone else does for a living. They are all anonymous, on holiday.

That evening, she and her son return. A wind is up, and the beach, turned cold, is abandoned while the guests feast indoors. She and her son are alone. He sits inside the Volkswagon sand sculpture. She takes a picture of him there on her disposable Kodak camera. Moments later, the two of them run about wildly in their cold, bare feet, kicking sand into the coming storm. Their devastation is anonymous.

What is the plan?

Always, her husband would ask on a Saturday morning when he woke, "What's the plan today?" looking to her for guidance. Through seven years of marriage they had drifted along parallel lines, the interval of a seventh apart. She has taken her notes with her, is supposed to return with a proposal for how to unravel those years financially, how to effect the separation. Instead, she stares blankly at the ocean. At night, she sleeps.

The next day, the beach remains deserted, and she and her son take their blankets down from the room and curl up together on a single beach chair. She reads out loud all day from their temporary encampment, from a child's version of *The Odyssey*. By day's end, they come to the part just after Odysseus's return, where Penelope, ever sceptical, suggests her servant move their bed into another room while she sleeps this last night on her lonely couch. Odysseus roars with laughter: "Ah, Penelope, you and I alone know the secret of our bed. I myself built it around a living olive tree. Rather than cut it down, I carved the trunk and used it as one of the legs for our bed. Even now that leg is firmly rooted."

I want to thank you, she had said to her husband quietly. He looked up at her, bemused, and then the smile hardened into anger as her words rolled toward him. *I want to thank you for not begging me to stay. I am a loyal woman. It would have taken so very little. I would have stayed. I am glad I did not give a lifetime to learn just how little I really meant to you. How little you cared. How easily you could let go.*

"Penelope suddenly burst into uncontrollable sobbing. Odysseus emerged from the shadows. Penelope did not hesitate this time. She ran into his welcoming arms."

"Momma, are you crying again?"

"Do you know olive trees can make olives after two thousand years? That is the secret of their marriage bed. That their love could endure like the living olive tree, longer than their lifetimes. That it can be possible."

"Momma, how will I bear it?" She had gone to his father's condominium to tuck in her son on the first night of their separation. In the bathroom, she washed his little face, contracted with pain, watched him square his heaving little shoulders and go out bravely to face his worst fear — separation from her. *You will bear it because you must, because you have no choice. I have done this to you.*

The Fourth Station of the Cross. Jesus meets his Mother:
Christ speaks: She counts my every wound. She shares my martyrdom—And I share hers. We hide no pain, no sorrow from each other's eyes. This is my Father's will.
I reply: To watch the pain of those we love is harder than to bear our own. I, too, must stand and watch the sufferings of my child. And I must let my child watch mine.

They are watching a blow hole in stone, her son singing quietly to himself, the way he is always singing, as if no one is listening. Just then, the group of little sharks her boy would have been part of, if he would agree to become a part of anything, rounds the corner. The face of the Englishwoman is there in the faces of her blond children, and then she herself emerges, bringing up the rear, with her camera. Instinctively, the boy falls silent, and gives way to the ten or so children who scramble over the rocks, collecting on their organized adventure.

Three Christmases ago, she was jamming at the piano with

her jazz singer neighbour, their boys playing together on the floor, when her boy unexpectedly stood on the footstool beside the piano and belted out a carol in perfect pitch, mock-snapping of his fingers in a bluesy style. *Silent night, oh silent night...* "Oh my God," the neighbour said. "You've got to do something about *that*." Where did it come from? She herself had the voice of a toad. Her own child had rejected her attempts at lullabies as a baby: *Boo-boo ears, do-do-do.* By six, she had him in a choir—like it or not, and mostly not— he had a responsibility to this gift. *When you sing, you make God so happy. You make me happy.* "Thank you," she would always say to him after every practice, "I needed that."

Now, as the sharks pass, she, who cannot sing if her life depended on it, starts singing from the song she learned with her son this Christmas:

> We rise again in the faces of our children
> We rise again in the voices of our song
> We rise again in the waves out on the ocean
> And then we rise again.

"Don't, Momma. *She'll* hear you."
"So what if she hears me? I want her to hear me."

> When the light goes dark
> With the forces of creation
> Across a stormy sky,
> We look to reincarnation to explain our lives
> As if a child, could tell us why....

It is the last day of the holiday. They take a bus to another beach with some of the other guests. There is a picnic on this beach, which was stormed out a few nights before, the night after mother and son destroyed the sand sculptures and were hidden in their complicity by the forces of creation. The Club Med staff has raked and cleared the beach. There is a barbeque, more organized games in which they do not participate, and shell picking. Only supposed to remove one, she takes a beach bagful. She and her son will dispense these as house gifts to anyone with courage or kindness enough to visit them in their separated grieving that next year. She feels buoyant, giddy, as on New Year's Day. Is it the wine at lunchtime, the sea, or simply being away from their suffering? Today she has seen her son smile for the first time in a week.

Just before they board the bus, the British woman approaches them. Kneeling unexpectedly before the boy, she says:

"You're a great kid. I just wanted you to know that. I hope you'll accept my apology."

"Yes, please," he says, as if receiving a second helping. Then, "Thank you. Me and my Momma really needed that."

Joy, Joy, why do I sing?
She could never remember the answer in the song. Is it for the *singing* itself? Or for the *joy*? The question in one being with the answer.

Joy, joy, why do I sing? Why do I, do I? Why do I do anything? Joy, joy, why am I? Why do I sing?

epilogue

After all, what was music, what was a prelude, a sonata, a minuet? What were all those forms, those structures containing the content within barlines and keys? No one's private invention: form was all of man's intuition of some unity, his recognition that there was proportion, an intelligible, if obscure, harmony of systems in the physical world.

Danielle felt a sudden elation. This, somehow, was the meaning: not that there was no meaning, or that there was one meaning, one great, overwhelming revelation, but that there were these little glimpses, these little illuminations of some primal link between a bullfrog and Bach....

DARLENE MADOTT is a Toronto lawyer and writer. She won the 2002 Anne & Henry Paolucci Prize for Italian American Writing in Fiction. She was first published by Women's Press in 1998, in *Curaggia*, a collection of writing by women of Italian descent. Madott has another short story collection, *Bottled Roses*, and has also been published in several anthologies.